Rogue Protocol

ALSO BY MARTHA WELLS

THE MURDERBOT DIARIES
All Systems Red
Artificial Condition

BOOKS OF THE RAKSURA
The Cloud Roads
The Serpent Sea
The Siren Depths
The Edge of Worlds
The Harbors of the Sun
Stories of the Raksura: Volume I (short fiction)
Stories of the Raksura: Volume II (short fiction)

THE FALL OF ILE-RIEN TRILOGY
The Wizard Hunters
The Ships of Air
The Gate of Gods

STANDALONE ILE-RIEN BOOKS
The Element of Fire
The Death of the Necromancer
Between Worlds: the Collected Ile-Rien and Cineth Stories

YA NOVELS
Emilie and the Hollow World
Emilie and the Sky World
Blade Singer (with Aaron de Orive)

TIE-IN NOVELS
Stargate Atlantis: Reliquary
Stargate Atlantis: Entanglement
Star Wars: Razor's Edge

City of Bones
Wheel of the Infinite

ROGUE PROTOCOL

THE MURDERBOT DIARIES

MARTHA WELLS

A TOM DOHERTY ASSOCIATES BOOK
NEW YORK

This is a work of fiction. All of the characters, organizations, and events portrayed in this novel are either products of the author's imagination or are used fictitiously.

ROGUE PROTOCOL

Copyright © 2018 by Martha Wells

All rights reserved.

Edited by Lee Harris

A Tor.com Book
Published by Tom Doherty Associates
175 Fifth Avenue
New York, NY 10010

www.tor-forge.com

Tor® is a registered trademark of Macmillan Publishing Group, LLC.

The Library of Congress Cataloging-in-Publication
Data is available upon request.

ISBN 978-1-250-19178-6 (hardcover)
ISBN 978-1-250-18543-3 (ebook)

Our books may be purchased in bulk for promotional, educational, or business use. Please contact your local bookseller or the Macmillan Corporate and Premium Sales Department at 1-800-221-7945, extension 5442, or by email at MacmillanSpecialMarkets@macmillan.com.

First Edition: August 2018

Printed in the United States of America

17 16 15

Rogue Protocol

Chapter One

I HAVE THE WORST luck with bot-driven transports.

The first one had let me stow away in exchange for my collection of media files, with no ulterior motives, and had been so focused on its function that there had been hardly more communication between us than you'd have with a hauler bot. For the duration of the trip I had been alone with my media storage, just the way I like it. It had spoiled me into thinking all bot transports would be like that.

Then there was Asshole Research Transport. ART's official designation was deep space research vessel. At various points in our relationship, ART had threatened to kill me, watched my favorite shows with me, given me a body configuration change, provided excellent tactical support, talked me into pretending to be an augmented human security consultant, saved my clients' lives, and had cleaned up after me when I had to murder some humans. (They were bad humans.) I really missed ART.

Then there was this transport.

It was also bot-driven, no crew, but it carried passengers,

mostly minimum to moderately skilled tech workers, human and augmented human, traveling to and from transit stations on temporary work contracts. This was not an ideal situation for me, but it was the only transport going in the right direction.

Like bot-transports that were not ART, it communicated in images and had allowed me onboard in exchange for a copy of my stored media. Because the manifest was in the transport's feed and so available to the other passengers, I asked it to list me for the duration of the voyage in case anybody checked. There was a field in the passenger form for occupation and in a moment of weakness, I told it I was a security consultant.

Transport decided that meant it could use me as onboard security and started alerting me to problems among the passengers. I was an idiot and started responding. No, I don't know why, either. Maybe because it was what I was constructed to do and it must be written into the DNA that controls my organic parts. (There needs to be an error code that means "I received your request but decided to ignore you.")

Initially, it had been pretty easy. ("If you bother her again I will break every individual bone in your hand and arm. It will take about an hour.") Then it had gotten more complicated as even the passengers who liked each other started to get into fights. I spent a lot of time (valuable time I could have been viewing/reading my saved entertainment media) arbitrating arguments I didn't give a shit about.

Now it was the last cycle of the trip, all of us somehow having managed to survive, and I was heading into the mess compartment to break up yet another fight between idiot humans.

Transport didn't have drones, but it did have a limited range of security cameras, so I knew the positions of everybody in the galley/mess area before the door slid open. I strode across the room, through the maze of shouting humans and overturned tables and chairs, and stepped between the two combatants. One had picked up a food utensil as a weapon and in one careful non-finger-ripping-off twist I had it, instead.

You would think the person they knew as a security consultant slamming in and disarming one of them would cause everyone to stop and reassess their priorities in this situation, but oh, you would be wrong. They staggered back, still screaming profanity at each other. The others in the room switched from shouting profanity at the combatants to shouting at me, all trying to tell me different versions of what had happened. I yelled, "Shut up!"

(The good thing about pretending to be an augmented human security consultant instead of a construct SecUnit is that you can tell the humans to shut up.)

Everybody shut up.

Then, still breathing hard, Ayres said, "Consultant Rin, I thought you said you didn't want to come back up here—"

The other one, Elbik, was pointing dramatically. "Consultant Rin, he said he was going to—"

I'd had Transport list my name as Rin on the manifest though I'd used Eden at RaviHyral. I was fairly certain RaviHyral transit station security had no reason to associate that identity with any sudden deaths taking place on a private shuttle, and even if they had, wouldn't pursue anyone out of their jurisdiction unless contracted to. But it had seemed best to change it.

The others, starting to come out from behind tables and hastily assembled chair barricades, all tried to chime in, and there was more pointing and shouting. This was typical. (If it wasn't for the shows I download from the entertainment feed, I would have thought the only way most humans knew how to communicate was by pointing and shouting.)

The objective twenty-six cycles of the journey had felt like a subjective two hundred and thirty, at least. I had tried to distract them. I had copied all my visual media into Transport's passenger-accessible system so it could be played on all their display surfaces, which at least kept the crying to a minimum (for children and adults). And, granted, the fighting had decreased dramatically after the first time I pinned someone to a wall with one hand and established a clear set of rules. (Rule Number One: do not touch Security Consultant Rin.) But even that usually left me standing there helplessly listening to their problems and their grievances against each other, against various corporations they had been fucked over by (yeah, tell me about it), and against existence in general. Yes, listening to it was excruciating.

Today, I said, "I don't care."

Everybody shut up again.

I continued, "We have, at most, six hours left before this transport will dock. After that, you can do whatever you want to each other."

That didn't work, they still had to tell me about what had caused the latest fight. (I don't remember what it was, I deleted it from memory as soon as I could get out of the room.)

They were all annoying and deeply inadequate humans, but I didn't want to kill them. Okay, maybe a little.

A SecUnit's job is to protect its clients from anything that wants to kill or hurt them, and to gently discourage them from killing, maiming, etc., each other. The reason why they were trying to kill, maim, etc., each other wasn't the SecUnit's problem, it was for the humans' supervisor to deal with. (Or to willfully ignore until the whole project devolved into a giant clusterfuck and your SecUnit prayed for the sweet relief of a massive accidental explosive decompression, not that I'm speaking from experience or anything.)

But here on this transport, there was no supervisor, just me. And I knew where they were going, and they knew where they were going, even if they were pretending all their anger and frustration was caused by Vinigo or Eva taking an extra simulated fruit pac. So I listened to them a lot and pretended to be launching major investigations into incidents like who left a cracker wrapper in the galley restroom sink.

They were heading to a labor installation on some shitshow world. Ayres told me they had all sold their personal labor for a twenty-year hitch, with a big payout at the end. He was aware it was a terrible deal, but it was better than their other options. The labor contract included shelter, but charged a percentage for everything else, like food consumed, energy use, and any medical care, including preventative.

(I know. Ratthi had said using constructs was slavery but at least I hadn't had to pay the company for my repair, maintenance, ammo, and armor. Of course, nobody had asked me if I wanted to be a SecUnit, but that's a whole different metaphor.)

(Note to self: look up definition of metaphor.)

I had asked Ayres if the twenty years was measured by

the planetary calendar or the proprietary calendar of the corporation who maintained the planet, or the Corporation Rim Recommended Standard, or what? He didn't know, and hadn't understood why it mattered.

Yeah, that was why I was trying not to get attached to any of them.

I would never have picked this transport if I had a choice, but it had been the only one going to the transit station that was the connection to my next destination. I was trying to get to a place called Milu, outside the Corporation Rim.

I had made the decision after I left RaviHyral. At first, I had needed to move fast and put as much distance between myself and its transit station as possible. (See above, murdered humans.) I'd grabbed the first friendly cargo transport and after a seven-cycle trip I disembarked on a crowded transit hub, which was good, because crowds were easy to get lost in, and bad, because there were humans and augmented humans everywhere, all around me, looking at me, which was hell. (After meeting Ayres and the others, obviously my definition of hell changed.)

Also, I missed ART, and I even missed Tapan, and Maro and Rami. If you had to take care of humans, it was better to take care of small soft ones who were nice to you and thought you were great because you kept preventing them from being murdered. (They had only liked me because they thought I was an augmented human, but you can't have everything.)

After RaviHyral, I'd decided to stop screwing around and get out of the Corporation Rim, but I still had to plan my route. The schedules and feeds I needed hadn't been accessible on the transport, but now that we'd docked I was inundated with info, so I had to take some time to go through it all. Plus I had been at this hub for twenty-two minutes and I already desperately needed some quiet time. So I ducked into an automated transient service center and used some of the funds on my new hard currency card to pay for a private rest cubicle. It was just big enough to lay down in with my knapsack, but it was enough like a transport box to be vaguely comforting. I had spent a lot of great alone time in transport boxes, being shipped as freight to contracts. I thought a human had to be pretty tired to rest in here without screaming.

Once I was settled, I checked the station feeds for recently arrived newsbursts about DeltFall and GrayCris. I hit a story thread almost immediately. Lawsuits were underway, depositions in progress, and so on. It didn't look like there had been much change since I left RaviHyral, which was frustrating. That pesky SecUnit nobody wanted to talk about was still unaccounted for, so yay for that. It was hard to tell if the journalists thought somebody was hiding me or not. They didn't seem to want to speculate that I'd wandered off on my own. Then I hit an interview with Dr. Mensah, posted six cycles ago.

It was unexpectedly good to see her again. I increased magnification for a better look and decided she seemed tired. I couldn't tell where she was from the video background and a quick scan of the interview content didn't mention it. I hoped she was back on Preservation; if she was still on Port FreeCommerce I hoped they had contracted decent security. But knowing how she felt about SecUnits (the whole "it's slavery" thing) I doubted she had. Even without a MedSystem on my feed, I could tell there were changes in the skin around her eyes that indicated a lack of sleep verging on chronic.

I felt a little guilty, sort of, almost. Something was wrong, and I hoped it wasn't about me. It wasn't her fault I'd escaped, and I hoped they weren't trying to hold her responsible for, you know, releasing a rogue SecUnit with a record of past mass murder onto an unsuspecting population. Granted, that hadn't been her intention. She had meant to ship me home to Preservation, where she would have, I don't know, civilized me, or educated me, or something. I was vague on the details. The only thing I knew for certain was that Preservation didn't need SecUnits, and their idea of a SecUnit being considered a free agent meant I'd have a human "guardian." (In other places they just call that your owner.)

I reviewed the content again. The investigation of GrayCris being conducted by the news agencies was turning up other incidents that suggested the attack on DeltFall was more business as usual for them than an aberration. (This is my surprised face.) GrayCris had been collecting complaints for a long time about sketchy contracts and exclusive-use deals on various sites, including a potential terraforming project outside the Corporation Rim that had been abandoned, though nobody knew why. Fucking up a planet, even part of a planet, for no reason was kind of a big deal, and I was surprised they had gotten away with it. Okay, no, I wasn't surprised.

The journalist asked Dr. Mensah about that last one, and she said, "After what I saw of GrayCris, I intend to urge the Preservation Council to join the formal call to investigate the situation at Milu. A failed terraforming attempt is a tragic waste of both resources and the natural surface of a planet, but GrayCris has refused to explain their actions."

The journalist had tagged an infobar to Mensah's statement, with some commentary about a small company from outside the Corporation Rim which had recently filed to take possession of GrayCris' abandoned terraform project. They had just set up an automated tractor array to prevent the derelict terraform facility from breaking up in the atmosphere, and were supposed to start assessments soon.

The commentary got all dramatic then, wondering what the assessment team would find.

I laid there, flicking through feeds and schedules, and decided I thought I knew what the assessment team would find.

The reason I was wandering free and Dr. Mensah was on the news was because GrayCris had been willing to kill a whole bunch of helpless human researchers for exclusive access to alien remnants, the mineral and possibly biological remains of a sentient alien civilization left in the soil of our survey area. I knew a lot more about it now, after listening to Tapan and the others talk about their code for identifying strange synthetics, and because I'd downloaded a book on it and read it between episodes of my shows. There were tons of agreements between political and corporate entities, inside and outside the Corporation Rim, dealing with alien remnants. Basically you weren't supposed to touch them without a lot of special certifications and maybe not even then.

When I had left Port FreeCommerce, the assumption was that GrayCris had wanted unimpeded access to those remnants. Presumably, GrayCris would have set up a mining operation or colony build or some other kind of massive project as cover while they recovered and studied the remnants.

So what if the terraform facility at Milu was just a

successful cover for a mining or recovery operation for alien remnants or strange synthetics or both? GrayCris had finished the recovery and pretended to abandon the terraform that had never actually been in progress. With the facility derelict, it would eventually break up in the atmosphere, taking all the evidence with it.

If Dr. Mensah had proof of that, the investigation against GrayCris would get a lot more interesting. Maybe so interesting that the journalists would forget all about that stray SecUnit. And then Dr. Mensah wouldn't be needed on Port FreeCommerce and she could go back to Preservation where it was safe and I could stop worrying about her.

Getting proof wouldn't be hard, I thought. Humans always think they've covered their tracks and deleted their data, but they're wrong a lot. So . . . maybe I should do that. I could go to Milu and take whatever data I collected and send it to Dr. Mensah, either to wherever she was staying at Port FreeCommerce or to her home on Preservation.

I picked up the hub feed again and changed my queries to search for transports to Milu, but there was nothing on the public schedule for this transit station. I widened my search, checking other connected transit stations. All I could find was an old transportation advisory, tagged forty cycles ago, when the news said the terraform facility had been declared abandoned after the local transit station had registered a lengthy period of inactivity. It said the cargo routes to Milu were discontinued, all except for the route originating at HaveRatton Station, which was on the edge of the Corporation Rim. I couldn't get any updated information about transports going to Milu from HaveRatton, except some vague reports that some had still been in operation at some point.

I might not be able to get to Milu without my own ship, and that wasn't going to happen. I have a training module for hoppers and other planetary aircraft, but not shuttles or transports or anything. I'd have to steal a ship and a bot pilot, and that would just be getting too complicated, even for me.

But HaveRatton was a main hub for transports heading outside the Corporation Rim and I could choose hundreds of destinations from there. So even if the Milu plan turned out to be a bust, it wouldn't be a wasted trip.

The next transport leaving directly for HaveRatton was listed as cargo and passenger, and that's how I ended up with Ayres and his bunch of contract-labor-bound idiots.

After breaking up the latest fight in the mess, and trying to end my short-lived career as a relationship counselor for desperate humans, I went to hide in my bunkspace. When we came through the wormhole and started to approach HaveRatton, I picked up the station feed.

I needed to get the schedules as soon as possible, and I was also looking forward to a chance to download new media. The latest new show I was watching had started out good but turned annoying. It was about a pre-terraform survey (on a planet with completely the wrong profile for terraforming anyway, but I didn't care about that part) that turned into a battle for survival against hostile fauna and mutant raiders. But the humans were too helpless to make it interesting and they were all getting killed. I could tell it was headed toward a depressing ending, and I just wasn't in the mood. It was especially annoying because I could see how the addition of a heroic SecUnit and maybe some interesting alien remnants could have turned it into a great adventure story.

And there was no way their bond company would have guaranteed the survey without some kind of professional security. That was unrealistic. Heroic SecUnits were unrealistic, too, but like I had told ART, there's the right kind of unrealistic and the wrong kind of unrealistic.

I had stopped watching it when the mutants dragged off the group's biologist to eat him. Seriously, this was exactly the kind of situation I was designed to prevent.

Thinking about the probable fate of Transport's passengers put me out of the mood, too. I didn't want to see helpless humans. I'd rather see smart ones rescuing each other.

I sorted through indices of available info, then started new downloads and queried the schedules and transport guide for ways to get to Milu.

Nothing this cycle, nothing the next. Even when I widened the search to thirty cycles from now. Well, that was possibly a problem.

I had been thinking about my plan a lot in between bouts of passenger-wrangling, and now I hated to give it up; I really wanted to hurt GrayCris, and if I couldn't do it with explosive projectiles, this was the next best way. Maybe the schedules hadn't been updated; humans are so fucking unreliable when it comes to maintaining data. As we slowed for final approach and docking, I searched the station's public destination catalog, and yeah, Milu was listed. As usual, an independent company operated the transit station, so it was listed as still active even after the facility had been abandoned. The population of the station was floating and under one hundred at most.

Floating was good as it meant there were few permanent residents; people came and went constantly. But under a hundred was bad. Even if I could get there, with no legitimate reason to be there, I'd have to make sure no one saw me.

ART had altered my configuration so scans wouldn't read me as a SecUnit, and I had written myself some code to make sure I behaved more like a human or augmented human. (Mostly randomizing my movements and breathing.) But I had to avoid other SecUnits, and it was best to avoid humans (like deployment center personnel) who had seen SecUnits without armor. GrayCris contracted for SecUnits in the Corporation Rim, and they might have used them on the Milu station, too. GrayCris was supposed to have removed any offices from the transit station when they abandoned the facility, but the humans who were still there might have seen their SecUnits. It was a calculated risk, which meant I was doing it even though I knew it could be like shooting myself in the knee joint.

I could have given up on the whole idea. There were transports leaving for destinations far away from Corporate territory, destinations I didn't know anything about. But I was tired of pretending to be human. I needed a break.

I tried the schedule for privately owned ships and didn't see any marked for Milu. But there were several ships scheduled to leave in the next cycle or so with no listed destination. One was a small bot-piloted cargo ship that was just large enough to carry supplies for about one hundred to one hundred-fifty humans for one hundred-plus cycles. I checked its history in the knowledge base and saw that it left and returned on a regular schedule. It could be a private contractor supplying Milu station, and not listed on the schedule because they didn't want any random humans trying to go there until the terraforming facility debacle had been sorted out.

The cargo ship had actually been scheduled to leave eighteen cycles ago, but had requested a hold. Six transports of varying sizes and points of origin were arriving on HaveRatton at the same time as my transport. The supply ship might have been waiting for one of those, if it was fulfilling specific cargo orders. It might have been waiting for a repair.

To find out more, I'd have to ask in person.

Chapter Two

ONCE TRANSPORT COMPLETED DOCKING protocols, I climbed out of my bunk, collected my knapsack (I had a few things in it but mostly it was just so I could look more like a human traveler), and took a shortcut down the maintenance shaft to the passenger lock. The others would be going out through the cargo lock, into a transport module that a cargo lifter would tow to the ship taking them to their new home. This was billed as for their convenience, but their contractor wouldn't want them to walk through the station where they might change their minds and escape.

I didn't want to say goodbye. I couldn't save this many humans from where they were going, where they thought they wanted to go, but I didn't have to watch it, either.

I did say goodbye to Transport, which let me out of the lock and then deleted the record from its log. I could tell it was sad to see me go, but this wasn't a trip I'd be anxious to repeat.

I had practice at hacking different hub and ring security now, so it was much less nerve-racking to get past the weapon scans. SecUnits are designed to be mobile components of SecSystems, every kind of SecSystem, so the company can rent us to as many different clients as possible, even those with proprietary equipment. The trick to hacking a SecSystem is making it think you're supposed to be there, and the company had helpfully provided us with all the code necessary for that. Practice and terrifying necessity had made me good at altering it on the fly.

I did stop in the ring mall, at an automated kiosk that sold feed interfaces for non-augmented humans, portable display surfaces, and memory clips. The clips were for extra data storage, and were each about the size of a fingertip. They were used by humans who had to set up new systems or travel to places that didn't have the feed, or who wanted to store data somewhere that wasn't feed accessible. (Though company SecSystems had ways of reading them; clients sometimes tried to hide proprietary data on them.) I bought a set of clips with my hard currency card. (I saw it still had plenty of money left on it; Tapan and the others must have paid me a lot.)

The private docks were never as busy as the public ones, with just a few humans heading in or out, and lots of hauler bots moving cargo. I scanned for drones as I crossed the embarkation floor, but there were only two there to monitor hauler bot activity. I found the supply ship's lock and pinged it to see if anyone was home. The bot pilot pinged back.

It was a lower-level bot, not high functioning enough to be bored while in dock or interested in the prospect of something to do. Like the transport bots I'd run into (ART was the exception) it communicated in images. Yes, it was a supply ship. Yes, it was going to Milu, it went to Milu on a forty-seven-cycle schedule. An update had come from transit control that it was to hold its departure, but it expected clearance sometime in the next two cycles. It was like talking to a recorded travelers' information ad.

But I figured I'd gotten lucky for once.

I made it think I had Port Authority authorization and asked it to let me board, and it did. Then I gently excised my entrance from its memory. As far as it was concerned, I had always been onboard. I didn't like to do it; I like to negotiate with bot pilots. But this one was so limited, I was afraid it was incapable of making a deal and sticking to it. I didn't want to risk it telling the Port Authority about me because it didn't understand why that was a bad idea.

I went down a short corridor into the main compartment and found the passage into the cargo and supply storage. It was small, just big enough for a console used to attach and remove the two cargo modules, and the lockers for onboard supplies. Both modules were already attached, so if the ship were waiting for cargo, one would have to be detached and reloaded. With the configuration of the crew area, that shouldn't affect me, though.

I used the time to search around, mostly because I was a little edgy and it's still programmed habit to patrol. Ship's repair drones followed me, attracted by a moving body where there wasn't supposed to be one, but without direction from Ship they didn't bother me. There were no private cabins, just a couple of bunks built against the bulkheads up on the control deck next to the pilot suite, and two more in cubbies behind the cargo station, next to the emergency MedSystem and a tiny restroom cubby. I didn't need it, and it would be a relief not to have to pretend to use it often enough to look human. Though I was getting used to having access to a human shower. Compared to a company security ready room, the accommodations were lavish. I settled on one of the bunks on the control deck and started sorting my new media.

(Okay, I should have realized that the pacs of bedding and other supplies in one of the lockers were probably there for a reason.)

After trying and rejecting a few newly downloaded shows, I started on a first episode that looked promising. It took place in an alt-world with magic and improbable talking weapons. (Improbable because I was a talking weapon and I knew how people felt about me.)

Some twenty or so hours later, I was still deep in the show, and enjoying my human-free vacation. Fortunately, when the life support cycled on, I felt the air pressure increase. (I don't need much air, and can always go into hibernation mode if I run out, so the minimal atmosphere on automated transports is fine for me.)

I paused the show and sat up. I queried the bot pilot and asked if anyone was coming aboard. Yes, the two passengers were coming aboard, and it had received an update from transit authority that it was now cleared to file for a departure time.

Another one of those "oh shit" moments.

I'd searched the ship already, at least, so I had a couple of likely spots in mind. I rolled off the bunk, remembered to grab my bag, dropped down the vertical passage to the main compartment. I crossed the compartment and went down the passage to the cargo area. I picked the locker that was the least accessible, and shifted the contents around until I could squeeze myself into the back, the supply pacs screening me from view. I cozied up to the bot pilot and reminded it I was supposed to be here and there was no need to mention me to anybody else, including its passengers and the Port Authority. It didn't have any security cameras (transports not controlled by corporate political entities rarely do) but it did have the drones. With their scanners, I had a good view of all the interior compartments, once I filtered out the maintenance data I didn't need.

Sixteen minutes later, the lock cycled and two passengers came aboard. Two augmented humans, carrying traveling packs and a couple of cases I recognized immediately. Combat gear, including armor and weapons.

Huh. Bots were more common for combat than humans for the same reason SecUnits were more common for security contracts: if we don't follow orders, we get our brains fried. But there were joint corporate and other political entity treaties about the use of combat bots. (Though everybody seemed to find ways around that. It was a pretty common plot on some of the serials from outside the Corporation Rim.)

I listened in with the drones and Ship's feed, but the two humans didn't talk much, just stowing their gear with occasional remarks to each other. From their feed signatures, I knew their names were Wilken and Gerth. It was too much to expect that they would chat about why they were going to Milu, but there were ways.

As a SecUnit, a large part of my function was helping the company record everything my clients did and said so the company could data mine it and sell anything worthwhile. (They say good security comes at a price and the company takes that literally.) Most of the recordings are just junk that gets deleted, but it has to be analyzed first and the good bits pulled out. Normally this is done in conjunction with a SecSystem, but I can do it alone and I still have all the code for it. It was taking up space in my storage that could have been used for media, but it was also something I couldn't replace on the fly.

While the two humans pulled some supply pacs from the locker I wasn't in and got settled, I adjusted the drones' code to let them record. Once I collected enough data, I could start the analysis in background.

As Ship disengaged from the lock and started its trip to Milu, I was already watching my new show again.

It took twenty cycles by Ship's local time to get to Milu.

I hadn't expected it to bother me. I've been in transport boxes and cubicles for much longer, and a lot of those trips were before I hacked my governor module and started downloading media. But I wasn't used to traveling as cargo anymore, even with new shows, serials, and several hundred books to go through. The transient rest tube hadn't bothered me, and I had spent three other transport trips, including the one with ART, mostly without moving. I wasn't sure what the difference was. Okay, maybe I was sure: in all the other spaces, I'd had the ability to move whenever I wanted.

Whatever, it was a relief when Ship reported that it was on approach to Milu. Two minutes later I realized I was picking up the station feed, but there was nothing on it.

Usually there's traffic and docking information, potential navigation hazards, travelers' news, that kind of thing, but here there was nothing. I checked with Ship, who reported that there was no other traffic on approach, but this matched with its previous experiences docking at this station. (I had watched a serial once that featured a dead haunted station and okay, that was unlikely, but it's better to make sure.)

The silence was still weirdly unnerving. The station was triangle-shaped and smaller than RaviHyral. The scan showed two ships in dock and a scatter of shuttles, a fraction of its capacity.

Ship had moved into docking position before I finally heard anything on the feed. The welcome message sounded normal enough, but the station index looked like the info system had glitched. There was a list of businesses and services, but each entry had been updated with a closed/inactive notice. So the place might not be haunted, but it was teetering on the edge of dead/inactive status.

While I waited for Ship to finish docking, I checked the results of my analysis. Wilken and Gerth were security consultants, hired by a fact-finding research group contracted by GoodNightLander Independent. GI had filed the abandonment markers on GrayCris' deserted terraforming facility, and set up the tractor array to protect it from disintegration, and now they were starting the process to take formal possession. The research group's job was to go into the facility and to make a report on its status.

This was exactly the kind of contract that bond companies supply SecUnits for, the kind of contract I had done more times than I still had in my memory. But from Wilken and Gerth's conversations over the past twenty cycles, it was clear there was no bond company, no SecUnits. I tried not to take it personally.

(If a bond company with SecUnit security had been involved, I would have had to abort this ... whatever it was I was doing. The change in my configuration would fool scans but not another SecUnit, and any Unit that detected me would report it to their HubSystem immediately. I sure as hell would have reported me. Rogue SecUnits are fucking dangerous, trust me on that.)

While I was waiting for Ship to finish its docking procedure, I figured the clanking of the docking process would mask any noise from small movements. I pulled my knapsack around, opened the skin of my right arm where it met the edge of my energy weapon, and inserted all the memory clips I'd bought into the space. They felt weird and bulky, but I'd get used to it. I was going to leave my knapsack here in the locker.

We docked, and Wilken and Gerth gathered their gear and went out the airlock into the station. As I unpacked myself from the locker, I used the station's public feed to hack its security system. Most of the cameras weren't active, and the scans were checking exclusively for environmental safety and damage detection. They were more worried about their equipment failing than people attempting theft or sabotage, but maybe that was because there weren't that many people.

Once I'd repacked the locker and made sure I hadn't left any traces of my presence, I poked around a little to see if the humans had left anything behind. No luck. I hesitated, considering Ship's drones. With not many cameras to rely on, drones would be nice. But the repair drones were much larger than the ones I was used to working with, mostly to accommodate the little arms and hands they needed for maintenance. I decided depriving Ship of any of them wasn't worth it.

I did make a few other adjustments. I had Ship note itself in the port's schedule as under maintenance and made it think it needed my authorization to leave. Since Ship took care of itself and the company that owned it didn't even have so much as a kiosk in this system, I didn't think anybody would bother to check on it as long as it didn't outstay its schedule by more than a few cycles. With so few ships in dock, I didn't want to get stuck here.

When I cycled through Ship's lock, the embarkation area was empty. A lack of adequate lighting created lots of shadows, which didn't disguise the scuff marks and stains on the big floor panels. A lone food wrapper drifted along in the breeze from the air recirc, like they weren't even running the cleaners anymore. There were no drones, no hauler bots. There were two big bot-piloted lifters outside now removing Ship's cargo modules for transfer, and I was glad to be able to hear them banging around out there and sending each other data over the station's mostly silent feed. I don't like having to navigate halls crowded with humans staring at me and making eye contact, but the opposite was oddly just as creepy.

I found Gerth and Wilken on one of the few working security cameras and started after them. They were heading down the embarkation hall, not up to the habitation levels. There was no tourist map info in the feed, but hacking the cameras gave me access to the station's maintenance system and I pulled a schematic from there. All the areas except for what was essential for minimum station operation were shut down. I wondered if GoodNightLander Independent's petition for reclamation from abandonment was popular up here on the transit station. I already didn't like this place much and I didn't have to live here.

I have code for freezing cameras and deleting myself from them that I've used under much more difficult circumstances, and I altered it to work with the station's proprietary security system. Though really, the biggest danger was a human spotting me from down the terminal and thinking, *Hey, who's that?* Fortunately the station was mostly dark.

I trailed Wilken and Gerth to the end of the embarkation hall and up the ramp toward what the schematic said was the Port Authority/Cargo Control offices.

As I passed the lock junction at the top of the ramp something bright and colorful popped up right in front of me and I nearly screamed. It was an ad for a cargo service, created by marker paint on the floor that reacted to movement. It threw a little video into the feed, too, just in case you somehow missed the glowing thing in your face. Usually these markers are only used for emergency procedures because they work even if the power is down. I had never seen them used for ads before. The whole point of markers was that they were the only thing visible in a power outage so it would be easy to see them. It was hard enough trying to get stupid humans to follow the markers to safety without ads popping up obscuring the emergency route—

I reminded myself it wasn't my job to get humans to safety anymore.

I still hated the marker ads.

I checked the cameras again and saw Wilken and Gerth had found signs of life in the Port Authority area. They stood outside an office center with three levels of bubble windows looking out over what should be the station mall. It was an open plaza area with a couple of tube transports arcing overhead, and a big globular display that was currently on standby hovering in the air. It was surrounded by multi-levels of dark shadowy occupation blocks and empty fronts for places that should be cafés, hotels, cargo brokers, transit offices, tech shops, and so on. Much of it looked unfinished, like no one had ever moved in, and the rest had closed, nothing left behind but a few stray floating display surfaces.

I turned into a corridor that would have led away from the Port Authority district into the main habitation block, if there had been one. I walked in the near-darkness until I found an empty cubby prepared for something that had never been installed, and crouched down inside it. I could monitor the cameras now without worrying about any random station personnel spotting me. A maintenance/weapons scanner drone brushed my feed, and I grabbed it and got control. It was on a desultory patrol outside the PA offices and I used it to give me better views and audio than the static security camera.

Wilken and Gerth were talking to two new humans. There was also a human-form bot standing nearby. I hadn't seen one in a while in person, just on the entertainment feed. They aren't popular in corporation territory, because there's not a lot of things they can do that task-specific bots can't do better, and with the feed available their data storage and processing ability isn't that exciting. Unlike constructs, they don't have any cloned human tissue, so they're just a bare metal bot-body that can pick up heavy things, except not as well as a hauler bot or any other kind of cargo lifter.

In some entertainment media I had seen, they were used to portray the evil rogue SecUnits who menaced the main characters. Not that I was annoyed by that or anything. It was actually good, because then humans who had never worked with SecUnits expected us to look like human-form bots, and not what we actually looked like. I wasn't annoyed at all. Not one bit.

I had to run back the drone's camera feed to catch up, I had been so busy conquering that burst of non-annoyance. The first new human said, "I'm Don Abene." She gestured to the other new human. "This is my colleague Hirune, and our assistant Miki." She hesitated. "Did the employment agent have time to brief you?"

"They said it was a bodyguard job." Wilken flicked a glance at the bot, which was apparently called Miki. It stood there with its head cocked, staring at her with big globe-like eyes. It was unusual for a human to introduce a bot, and that's putting it mildly. Gerth looked like she was struggling to keep her expression professionally blank. Wilken continued, "You're going down to the terraforming facility to make an initial assessment and your contract with GoodNightLander Independent requires a security team."

Abene nodded. "I'm hoping we won't actually need you. But the company that abandoned the facility didn't maintain the satellite monitoring, and no one has been inside since they left. We assume it's deserted, but there's no way to make sure."

"The agent said that was a potential problem," Gerth said. "The terraforming shield is preventing any off-site scanning?"

Hirune answered, "Yes. We know it's stable, because of the tractor array GI put into place, but that's all. The station's been monitoring the facility, but as you can see, there are no patrol vessels here."

She meant there was a possibility that raiders had moved into the facility. Except if they did that, they couldn't have been very good raiders, because they had ignored this station. Also, raiders tend to hit and run, and not hang around to live on a deteriorating terraforming facility.

Actually, with my experience in security, anybody who wanted to hang around and live on a deteriorating terraforming facility worried me a lot more than raiders.

Gerth and Wilken exchanged a look. Maybe the same thought had occurred to them. Wilken asked, "Is there a possibility there were active organisms in the facility when it was abandoned?"

"The biological matrices would have been sealed, and probably destroyed, before the staff left," Hirune said. She made a gesture, like flicking something away. "Even if they hadn't, there's very little chance that they could create any dangerous airborne contamination."

Wilken's expression remained professionally cool, but she persisted, "I meant something other than bacteria. Any organisms large enough to be a physical danger?"

Right, so even I knew more about terraforming than these two.

Hirune's face now had the blank, lip-biting expression I associated with humans trying not to show their feelings, especially the feeling that someone had said something unintentionally hilarious. (This is why it had been a struggle for me to give up armor; concealing facial expressions was hard, even for humans.)

Don Abene's eyes crinkled, but she made it seem more like she and Wilken were sharing a joke. "The matrix wouldn't be working with any organisms larger than bacteria. And there wouldn't really be any reason to bring any larger organisms up from the surface to the facility. Of course, we don't know that they didn't. So it's proper to exercise caution."

Wilken seemed to accept that, or at least didn't ask any more questions. It sort of made sense. It was a security consultant's job to be skeptical of their clients' assurances that everything was fine. (SecUnit clients, at least, only assured each other that everything was fine while you stared at the wall and waited for everything to go horribly wrong.)

Abene and Hirune walked the security consultants into the Port Authority now, where they had quarters with the skeleton station team. They were talking about a full briefing, team prep, and a departure time sixteen hours from now. Miki the human-form bot followed, then stopped. It turned, and looked up at the drone I was riding. Its head cocked and I could tell it was focusing in on the camera.

I let the drone go, its memory of the temporary takeover blanked. It sent a confused reorientation request to the PA's system, then wandered off back to its patrol route.

Miki didn't move, still staring into the dark with the opaque surface of its eyes. The feed was clear, it couldn't know I was here.

Then Miki sent a directionless ping. Just a call into the dark, checking to see if there was anyone out there who wanted to reply.

I checked myself for signal leakage, tightened my walls, and reminded myself to be careful. Just because the station feed was silent didn't mean no one was listening. The GI expedition would be running their feed off the systems equipment they brought with them, but someone on the station staff was giving the lifter bots orders and maybe still checking the security reports.

This place was so quiet, maybe Miki had picked up the marker ad I'd tripped. Maybe it had heard a whisper in the otherwise empty feed, and that was creepy enough it even bothered me. Finally, it turned and followed its owner into the PA complex.

I slipped out of the cubby and went down the dark hall to find a better hiding place.

I worked my way around through the maintenance passages and loading corridors, into an empty commercial slot not far from the Port Authority. After some careful work, I managed to get a view from the two security cameras inside the PA offices. Yes, two. It was weird to be around humans who didn't monitor everything everybody did constantly via Sec- or HubSystems or drones, and who relied on human supervisors. And one camera was in the central hub for the port traffic control and the other in a jury-rigged hub that was now acting as station control—the two places where if something went wrong, you needed to know right away; in other words, not the mess, restrooms, or private quarters. It was almost like nobody here cared what anybody said or did as long as they weren't trying to blow up the station or crash the lifter-bots. (After thousands of hours spent analyzing and deleting video of humans eating, having sex, performing hygiene, and eliminating excess bodily fluids, it was a relief, but still.)

Fortunately the GI expedition and the station staff seemed to be pretty casual with each other and I was able to catch enough conversation to hear that the first assessment would be a short one, just twelve hours on the facility for an initial estimate of its condition, then they would return to the station to analyze their findings, take a rest period, then head back. That sounded perfect. Twelve hours should be plenty of time for me to find what I needed.

I also heard what docking slot their ship was leaving from and when they were loading supplies aboard. I still needed help getting onto the expedition ship. But with none to few active systems to work through, I didn't have much choice.

I was going to have to make friends with the stupid pet robot.

Hi, Miki.

It answered immediately, *Hi! Who are you?*

I was using the address in the ping Miki had sent to establish a secure connection. Abene and the others had finished their prep and were taking a rest period before leaving for the terraforming facility. It gave me about three hours to seduce the robot. I didn't expect it to take that long.

I said, *I'm a security consultant. GoodNightLander Independent contracted with my security company to make sure your team completes their mission safely.* It tried to message Abene over the feed, and I blocked it. *You can't tell anyone I'm here.* I expected it to ask me how I had managed to take over its feed, how I had gotten onto the station. I thought I'd managed to anticipate most of the questions and had my answers ready.

It said, *But why not? I tell Don Abene everything. She's my friend.*

When I'd called it a pet robot, I honestly thought I was exaggerating. This was going to be even more annoying than I had anticipated, and I had anticipated a pretty high level of annoyance, maybe as high as 85 percent. Now I was looking at 90 percent, possibly 95 percent.

I managed to keep my reaction out of the feed. It wasn't easy. I said, *This has to be a secret, to keep Don Abene and the others safe. We can't risk anyone finding out about it.*

Okay, it said. I wasn't sure if it was serious. It couldn't be this easy. Maybe it was just going along until it had a chance to report me? But it said, *Promise me Don Abene and all my friends will be safe.*

I had the horrible feeling it was serious. I hadn't expected a bot on ART's level, but holy shit. Had the humans actually coded it to be childlike, or petlike, I guess? Or had its code developed that way on its own, responding to the way they treated it?

I hesitated, because while I would rather not see a group of humans killed (again), I wasn't their SecUnit, or even their pretend augmented human security consultant. It's hard to keep humans safe when you can't let them see you. But it was waiting, and I wanted it to trust me, and I said, *I promise.*

Okay. What's your name?

This caught me off guard. Bots don't have names, SecUnits don't have names. (I'd given myself a name, but it was private.) I used the name I'd given Ayres and the others, my poor dumb humans who had sold themselves to a company and by now probably understood just how bad a deal it was. *Rin. Security Consultant Rin.*

That's not your real name. I could tell through the feed it was genuinely confused. *It doesn't sound like you.*

Obviously Miki was getting more through the feed than I had assumed. That was all I needed. I had nothing prepared for this, and there sure as hell wasn't anything in my buffer that was remotely helpful. I defaulted to honesty (I know, I was surprised, too) and said, *Rin is what I want to be called. I don't tell anyone my real name.*

Okay. I understand, Rin. I won't tell anyone that you're here. I will be your friend and help Don Abene and our team.

Right. (I almost said, *Okay.*) I couldn't tell if that was a default answer or Miki was making me a solemn promise. Whatever, either it told the humans about me or it didn't, and if I was going to do this I had to assume it wouldn't. *Can you give me system access to your shuttle? I want to make sure it's safe.*

Okay. And the data came through the feed.

What they were calling a shuttle was actually a local space exploration/transit vehicle, with two levels of crew habitation areas plus a cargo hold that had been converted to bio lab space. It didn't have the drive to get through the wormhole, but it could go anyplace else around the system. No bot pilot, just the kind of minimal automatic pilot system that I was more used to seeing on atmospheric craft. Not that helpful if everyone capable of operating the ship's higher-level functions were injured or incapacitated. On the other hand, you couldn't deliver killware if there was no bot pilot to kill.

The shuttle had no independent SecSystem, either. I had seen on some media from outside the Corporation Rim that internal security was less of an issue there, that the focus was on potential external threats more than it was on policing your own people. I hadn't thought it was true, but it did mesh in with the lack of interest in monitoring the station staff in their private quarters. Also with the way my PreservationAux clients had behaved. It made me wonder what Preservation might be like, but I squelched that thought. It was probably a boring place where everybody would stare at SecUnits, just like everywhere else.

Miki was giving me full access, so I took a little tour via its memory of previous trips. It was a nice shuttle, way nicer than anything the company would have provided; even the upholstery was clean and repaired. It was another sign of GI's commitment to their reclamation project; it would have come here in a big transport's belly cargo module, or in tow via a dedicated supply hauler like Ship.

I would need to ride Miki's internal feed the way ART had ridden mine, though unlike ART I couldn't do it over the distance between a station and a planet. The good part was that there were plenty of places to hide onboard the shuttle, even without packing myself in a cabinet. The bad part was that I would have no systems to see through, no eyes and ears except for Miki.

Yeah, I was thrilled.

Miki, I'm going to need to use your systems to monitor your— I almost said *clients*. It took almost a full second for me to be able to use the word Miki wanted to hear. *—your friends. I need you to be my camera, and let me use your scanning ability. Sometimes I might need to speak through you, pretending to be you, to warn Don Abene and* *your friends about things I believe are dangerous. Can you let me do that?*

Obviously, with the access Miki had given me already, I could have taken Miki over, done what I wanted, and excised it all from its memory. I had done it to Ship, but Ship was a low-level bot and didn't have enough self-awareness to give a shit. Doing that to Miki ... But I didn't know what I would do if it said no.

Miki said, *Okay, I will do that, Consultant Rin. That sounds scary, but I want to make sure no one hurts my friends.*

This felt way too easy. I almost suspected a trap. Or ... *Miki, have you been directed to reply to every query with a yes?*

No, Consultant Rin, Miki said, and added, *amusement sigil 376=smile.*

Or Miki was a bot who had never been abused or lied to or treated with anything but indulgent kindness. It really thought its humans were its friends, because that's how they treated it.

I signaled Miki I would be withdrawing for one minute. I needed to have an emotion in private.

Chapter Three

I USED THE STATION'S hauler-bot delivery passage to get through the derelict mall and back down to the embarkation zone. The shuttle was docked in the Port Authority area and fortunately there was a working security camera. I was able to get a view of the area and see when it was clear. From Miki's feed I knew that two crew members were up on the control deck running a pre-flight check and the others were still in their station lab space doing their last check list.

I froze the camera's feed just long enough to sprint across the shadowy embarkation zone and reach the lock. I submitted the entry code Miki had supplied. The lock cycled open, letting out a breath of recycled air that my scan said was much cleaner than what was on the station. It sure smelled better. I stepped inside, closed the lock, and deleted my entry from the log.

I was listening in on Miki's feed connection with the human assessment team. I heard Kader, one of the two augmented human pilots up on the shuttle's flight deck, say, *Hirune, is that you?*

Hirune replied, *What? I'm still in the PA. We're about to come down.*

Oddness, I thought I heard the hatch open.

An entry's not in the log, the other pilot, Vibol, added. *I think your ears are confused.*

Now I have to check it out to prove you wrong, Kader told her.

I was already down the passage to the work space, past the bio labs to the supply storage. There was a slot for an onboard hauler bot, but since the cargo space had been converted to labs, the bot had been offloaded. It was more roomy than the supply locker on Ship, and at least I could sit on the deck and lean against the wall, even if I couldn't stretch my legs out. I didn't actually need to stretch, but it was nice. It was also completely dark, but with a lively feed in my head, that wasn't a problem.

Miki asked, *Are you okay, Consultant Rin?*

I checked again to make sure our connection was secure, that the humans couldn't hear it and none of the augmented humans could pick up an echo. It was, because I had control of Miki's feed, but I'd probably keep checking every time it talked to me because that was just the kind of cycle I was having. *I'm fine. You can call me Rin.* It was slightly less annoying than "Consultant Rin." It hadn't been annoying when Tapan, Rami, and Maro had called me Consultant, but ... I don't know, everything was annoying right now and I had no idea why.

Okay, Rin! Miki said. *We're friends, and friends call each other by name.*

Maybe I did know why.

I watched through Miki's eyes as it helped the expedition bring the last few pieces of their equipment and testing supplies down. They loaded it all through the airlock and stowed it away. I listened to them talk on the feed, and they seemed excited to be finally on their way. There were four researchers and two shuttle crew, all long-term employees of GoodNightLander Independent who had worked together before, who had been waiting impatiently here for their security detail to show up. Don Abene grabbed Miki's arms at one point and smiled into its camera. I was glad I hadn't made any attempt to control Miki's movements, because my recoil was so immediate and instinctive I whacked my head against the wall of my storage space.

(Nobody grabs SecUnits. I hadn't realized this was a perk until now.)

I'm still not good at telling human ages just by looking. Don Abene's warm brown skin was lined at the corners of her mouth and eyes, and her long dark hair had strands of white in it, but for all I knew it was a cosmetic choice. She laughed and her dark eyes crinkled. "We're finally going, Miki!"

"Hurray!" Miki said, and from inside its feed, I could see it was sincere.

Miki helped Hirune stow the protective suits, then defaulted to randomly following its human friends around as they stowed their personal gear. I suggested Miki walk out of the lab space and go to the storage area where Wilken and Gerth were unpacking their equipment. Miki didn't have a weapons scan nearly as sensitive as mine but its vision had magnification capabilities that mine didn't. (This is one of the differences between a security unit and a bot designed to help with scientific research.)

I asked it to take a good look at the cases the two security consultants were unpacking and it gave me a close-up view, breaking up the image into different angles as Gerth lifted her case into the storage locker. I'd wanted to do this aboard Ship, but they had stowed their gear too quickly, and asking a drone to inspect it would probably have drawn some unwanted attention. Gerth glanced at Miki, stowed the case, and said, "What are you looking at?"

I told Miki, *Say, "Don Abene wants me to ask you if you need any help stowing your gear."*

Miki cocked its head and repeated it verbatim, with the kind of perfect innocence only a perfectly innocent bot could manage.

Gerth smiled a little. "No, thanks, little bot," she said. Wilken chuckled.

"Little bot," seriously? (Somewhere there had to be a happy medium between being treated as a terrifying murder machine and being infantilized.) I prompted Miki to go back to its friends. As it retreated down the passage, it asked, *Rin, why did they not want us to see their cases?*

Not everybody wants a pet robot sticking its scanner into their business, but I was distracted and just said, *I'm not sure.* From the shapes, the cases held weapons, ammo, and a couple of high-end sets of self-adjusting armor, the kind I'd only seen in the media. The company had never given us armor that nice, though in its defense, our armor did get blasted off us at regular intervals. No drones, but then humans aren't good with security drones; it takes multi-track processing to direct them and most humans just can't do it without extensive augmentation. Even without drones, they looked like they were prepared for anything. *Maybe no reason.*

I was trying to decide if I should take the opportunity to steal anything if said opportunity should occur. The self-adjusting armor was incredibly tempting, and would be even better once I made some modifications to the code. But it was enough work to just get myself past the weapons scanners; bringing anything that bulky along was just going to make it more likely that I'd be caught.

Miki went up to the crew area below the control deck where Abene and Hirune sat with Brais and Ejiro. Kader and Vibol were just above us in the cockpit. The humans had turned a couple of the station chairs around to face the curved padded couch, and were watching the bubble of a floating display surface in the middle of the compartment. From the schematics on display, they were going over a proposed route through the facility. I was poking around carefully in their individual feeds, when Abene patted the seat next to her. "Sit down, Miki."

Miki sat next to her on the couch, and none of the other humans reacted. This was apparently perfectly normal.

"Are you excited to see the inside of the facility, Miki?" Hirune asked it, as she turned the schematic to a new angle. "I'm tired of just looking at maps of it."

"I'm excited!" Miki echoed. "We will do a good assessment, and then we can have a new assignment."

Ejiro laughed. "I hope it's that easy."

Brais said, "I don't care if it's easy or hard, at least we're moving! Miki was probably getting tired of playing Mus with us."

"I like games. I would play games all the time if we could," Miki said.

I had to withdraw back to my dark cubicle. I was having an emotion again. An angry one.

Before Dr. Mensah bought me, I could count the

number of times I sat on a human chair and it was never in front of clients.

I don't even know why I was reacting this way. Was I jealous of a human-form bot? I didn't want to be a pet robot, that's why I'd left Dr. Mensah and the others. (Not that Mensah had said she wanted a pet SecUnit. I don't think she wanted a SecUnit at all.) What did Miki have that I wanted? I had no idea. I didn't know what I wanted.

And yes, I know that was probably a big part of the problem right there.

I stepped back into Miki's feed. Don Abene was saying, "—keep in mind that your experience with humans is limited. We think of you as one of our family, but to others, you are a stranger. That's probably why our security team didn't want you to look at their things."

Uh-oh. I ran back Miki's camera to pick up the part of the conversation I'd missed. Miki had asked Abene why Gerth had reacted that way when it had looked at her and Wilken's cases. Fortunately, Abene had gotten distracted trying to answer the question while still looking over the facility's schematic, and hadn't asked why Miki had gone to see the security team. If she thought to ask about it, would Miki tell her about me? How would it answer that question?

I could take Miki over the way I'd originally planned, except its interactions with Abene and the others were incredibly complicated. I didn't think I could fake my way through that; my augmented human security consultant act had been hard enough to develop, and I wasn't trying to fool people who knew me. Or who I was pretending to be. Or whatever.

Trying not to sound nervous and/or enraged, I said, *Miki, remember you said you wouldn't tell Don Abene about me.*

I won't, Rin. Miki was so calm and complacent, my performance reliability dropped by 2 percent. *I promised.*

I managed to seethe silently. But part of Miki's coded behavior must include going to Don Abene when it had questions. I was going to need to make sure I answered its questions as thoroughly as possible; obviously "I don't know" wasn't going to cut it.

Hirune was asking Abene, "What do you think of our security team so far?"

Abene said, "I'm pleased, actually. They don't seem to know much about terraforming facilities, but that shouldn't matter."

It might, I thought. But SecUnit education modules were crap and all I knew about terraforming was what I had managed to absorb while completely not caring about it, so maybe I wasn't the best authority.

Through Miki's eyes, I saw Hirune glance at the other two, who were talking about calibrating something. She lowered her voice. "I suppose. With only two of them, they're not going to be much help against raiders."

Abene snorted. "If there are raiders, we're pulling out and heading back for the transit station immediately."

By the time you see them, it's too late for that.

My reaction must have gotten into the feed, because Miki asked anxiously, *You'll keep them safe, Rin?*

Yes, Miki, I told it, because that was my story and I was sticking to it.

Chapter Four

IN MIKI'S FEED I had access to a scan of the terraforming facility, superimposed with a schematic from the original specs. Yeah, I think I knew where to look for the evidence I wanted.

Through Miki's camera I saw the visual approaching on the shuttle's display. We had passed the tractor array already, still operating at optimal capacity according to the automated reports it was sending to the station.

The facility was a huge platform in the upper atmosphere, far larger than the station, larger than a full-sized transit ring. Most of that space was for the pods that contained the enormous engines that would actually control the terraforming process. There was no visual of the planet itself; the facility hung in a layer of perpetual storm. Swirling, towering clouds, filled with electrical discharges, obscured any view of the surface.

"We're seeing good levels on all the environmentals," Kader said from the cockpit, sharing an image of the readings through the feed. "Are you sure you want to go with full gear?"

I tensed, certain it was going to be the wrong answer. *Miki, tell her—* But Abene replied, "Yes, we'll go full safety protocol." That meant full suits, with filtering and emergency air supply, and some protection for vulnerable human bodies. "We'll keep to that until we can inspect the environmentals and take over facility control, then we'll reevaluate."

I relaxed. Then I reminded myself yet again that these weren't my clients.

Miki said, *It's okay, Rin. Don Abene is always cautious.*

I'd seen lots of dead cautious humans, but I wasn't going to say that to Miki.

Through Miki's eyes I watched Abene gear up for the first assessment walk-through. Kader and Vibol were staying on the ship, but Wilken and Gerth, plus Hirune and the two other researchers, Brais and Ejiro, were going with Abene and Miki.

Wilken exited the lock first, and her helmet cam sent the video into the feed. We had locked onto a passenger-only dock in the habitation pod and the embarkation area wasn't big enough to accommodate heavy equipment or standard hauler bots. Power was on but at minimal; emergency light bands glowed at the floor level, halfway up the wall, and at the top, but the larger overheads were off. It was enough light for the humans to see without the special filters in the helmet cameras.

Was it a good idea to board the facility here? The schematic showed a larger multi-use embarkation space on the level above us. This smaller loading zone could make the approach to the shuttle easier to defend, but it could also make it more difficult to get the team back into the shuttle if something went wrong.

It was hard to say if it was a bad judgment or not. There was always the fact that humans are lousy at security. I would have gone in first with a full deployment of drones, leaving the humans on the sealed shuttle. I would have evaluated the facility (i.e., made sure there weren't any unwanted visitors, by walking around as bait waiting for something to attack me) and only then brought the humans in. But don't mind me, it's not like I know what I'm doing or anything.

The camera in Wilken's armor sent video into the team feed as Wilken moved forward. She went through the lock and into the corridor, and I noted no damage, just a few scuffs and scrapes on walls and floor, signs of normal use. Abene, Hirune, Miki, and then Brais and Ejiro followed, with Gerth bringing up the rear. I split my attention into seven streams, one for each human's helmet camera plus Miki. I was listening in on the team feed and comm, but that was all coming through Miki, too. Abene said, "Miki, are you picking up anything?"

"No, Don Abene," Miki said. It was scanning for signal

activity from any resident systems. Since this facility had been built by GrayCris, I was expecting the kind of HubSystem and SecSystem I was used to, or something compatible. There were lots of security cameras everywhere, they just weren't active. Miki was right, there was nothing but dead air in here, no facility feed activity despite the power for lights and environmentals.

Maybe they thought the systems would be lonely if they were left active, Rin, Miki said. *What do you think?*

I wondered if ART had thought I was this stupid when it had been riding around in my head. Maybe, but the chances were good that if that had been the case, ART would have said so.

That might be true, I said, because I knew now if I didn't answer all Miki's questions it might accidentally rat me out to the nearest human. But then I remembered this place had been meant to collapse and burn up in the atmosphere before GI had put in the claim on it. I added, *GrayCris might have removed the central cores for the resident systems when they pulled out. They'd want to cut their losses.* Sec- and HubSystems that could run a facility this complex would be hugely expensive. I didn't know about GrayCris, but the company that owned me would never have left that much cash behind.

And Miki said, "Don Abene, maybe GrayCris removed

the central cores for the resident systems when they pulled out. They would want to cut their losses."

For fuck's sake.

"That makes sense," Hirune said. She had been poking at her comm, and added, "There's some interference, maybe shielding? I can't pick up the station traffic anymore, though I can still hear Kader and Vibol on our shuttle's feed."

Ejiro pulled a sample of the signal interference into his feed to study it. "Yes, we know the shielding's pretty heavy, probably due to the disturbances in the atmosphere." As if on cue, a burst of signal static blotted out the comm and feed for 1.3 seconds.

Heavy weather, Vibol commented over the comm. *Watch out for rain.*

The team chuckled, and Miki sent an amusement sigil into the team feed. Oh, a running joke, those aren't annoying at all. Wilken and Gerth ignored the byplay.

Ahead, Wilken stepped out of the corridor into a larger space, the scanner on her armor telling her it was empty of life signs. She paced around the circumference, clearing the room, then signaled the others to come in. This space wasn't labeled on the schematic but had decontam cubicles and environmental suits stored in racks against the walls. Again, no damage visible as the humans flashed their cameras around. Brais said, "Was this a clean facility? I thought the bio pod was separated and sealed. That's what it said in the schematic, wasn't it?"

"I'm sure that's the case," Hirune said. She checked a panel on the nearest decontam cubicle. It still had power, but the doors were all in the upright position. (Always a relief. Cubicles that something may be hiding in are no fun.) Hirune tried to get it to download a usage report to the feed, but its internal storage was empty.

I checked Kader and Vibol, who were both glued to their feeds, though Kader still had a channel open to station. There was some interference, but he was still getting pings and answers from the station Port Authority. It probably was the atmospheric shielding that was blocking the team inside from contact with the station.

Anyway, it was time to get moving. I slipped out of my storage cubby. I went down the corridor and cycled the lock, not allowing it to report the incident to its log. Kader had heard the lock open on the station when I boarded but this time was too occupied watching the team in the feed to notice.

I stepped out into the cooler facility air and let the lock close and seal.

The team had already moved out of the decontam room and headed toward the bio pod to check its status. I started down the corridor. I'd missed my armor off and on before this, usually when I was having to walk through large crowds of humans in transit rings. After being forced to do it to survive, plus traveling with Ayres and the others, I was sort of used to talking to humans and making eye contact, though I didn't like it.

This was the first time I missed my armor because I felt a physical threat.

I moved silently through the decontam room and took the exit corridor, then turned down the branch that led away from the bio pod, toward the geo pod. This corridor was the same as what I was seeing on Miki's camera and the team feed: no damage, no signs of hasty departure, just quiet corridors.

(I don't know why I expected to see damage and signs that the human staff had run for their lives; there was no indication that this was anything but a planned abandonment. Maybe I was thinking of RaviHyral again. You'd think once I'd seen the place, found out what had happened, the partial memories would fade. Not so much, it turned out.)

It shouldn't have been weird, but it was weird. I had Miki and the team backburnered, so I knew exactly where they were, and their voices filled the silence in the feed. But there was something about this place that made my human skin prickle under my clothes. I hated that.

I couldn't pin down what was bothering me. Scan was

negative, and this far away from the team there was no ambient sound except the whisper through the air system. Maybe it was the lack of security camera access, but I'd been in worse places with no cameras. Maybe it was something subliminal. Actually, it felt pretty liminal. Pro-liminal. Up-liminal? Whatever, there was no knowledge base here to look it up.

The team was proceeding down an outer corridor. On their left side, big bubble ports looked into a purple-gray cloud swirl in the storm, on the right were open passage locks leading down into the various engineering stacks. On a private channel to Miki, Abene said, *This place makes my skin shiver, Miki.*

I think so, too, Miki said. *Even though it's empty, it's like someone might step out in front of us at any moment.*

Well, Miki wasn't wrong. Something glittered in the air ahead, but when I reached the lift junction it was just an emergency marker display, floating below the ceiling and listing emergency exit procedures in thirty different languages. HubSystems offer continuous translation, and I'm guessing non-corporate political entities had something similar for their feeds, but in an emergency you'd want to make sure the instructions were clear even if the feed was down. There it was, cheerily doing its job in this empty hulk.

I tapped my private connection to Miki. *I'm about to*

use a lift, Miki. If your scan picks up the power fluctuation, please don't tell anyone.

Okay, Rin. Where are you going?

I have to look at the geo pod. It's part of my orders. The lift responded to a ping and arrived 1.5 seconds later, by which time I remembered that I'd told Miki my job was to provide extra security for the assessment team. Oops.

Fortunately, Miki understood about orders and it didn't occur to it to question me. *Be careful, Rin,* Miki said. *This place makes our skin shiver.*

I stepped into the lift and told it to go to the central geo pod. The door slid shut and it whooshed away. I tracked it on the schematic, as it curved past the giant bulbs used for atmosphere dispersal. I considered telling Miki that I was here to collect data on possible alien remnant violations by GrayCris. Nothing I was doing would hurt Abene or the team or GoodNightLander Independent, and I was already lying about so much. But Miki would tell Abene immediately, I knew it would. Not that her team wouldn't figure out on their own soon that something was sketchy about the terraforming facility. (Like the decontam room near the passenger lock; you don't need a clean facility for terraforming but you might if you were scavenging alien bio remnants.) But if Miki told Abene, she would ask how it knew, and I knew Miki would tell her about me. It wouldn't lie to a direct question.

Who knew being a heartless killing machine would present so many moral dilemmas.

(Yes, that was sarcasm.)

The lift stopped and the doors opened into another empty, quiet corridor. I followed it around and found the big hatchway into the main geological hub. It was a large semicircular space, with a section of ceiling that had been left clear. I'd seen the storm through Miki and the humans' cameras in the corridor on the way to the bio pod, but seeing it with my own eyes, no interface to interpret it, was different. The clouds were like a constantly moving structure, colors not so much swirling as in slow, ponderous motion. It was immense, and wrong, and terrible and beautiful all at the same time. I stood there for what I later clocked as twenty-two seconds, just staring.

Something must have bled over into the feed, because Miki said, *What are you looking at, Rin?*

That jolted me out of the spell. *Just the storm. The geo pod has a clear dome.*

Can I see?

I didn't know why not, so I made a copy of the visual, scrubbed any code that might identify me as a SecUnit from it, and passed it to Miki over the feed. *Pretty!* Miki said.

Miki ran the video a few times as it followed Abene down a ramp. They had passed a lift junction, but it wasn't big enough for all of them at once and Wilken sensibly refused to split the group. On the feed from Wilken's cam, I spotted hovering marker displays with the descriptor symbols for biological hazard potential; they were nearly there and I needed to get a move on. I wanted to be tucked up back in the shuttle and watching *Rise and Fall of Sanctuary Moon* by the time they finished their check of the bio pod.

The access consoles had been shut down and the data storage would have been removed entirely, which was way more secure than just a system delete. But that wasn't where I intended to look.

The schematic showed that the facility used diggers. (Actually geological manipulation semiautonomous . . . something something, apparently I deleted that out of permanent storage. Anyway, they aren't bots, they're just extensions of the geo systems.) The diggers have their own onboard storage for their procedures and tasks, but they also have scanning capability and they log what they find. I found and booted their interface console and yes, the diggers were still here, tucked under the geo pod, curled up in containers three times the size of our shuttle, inert without their parent system.

With the interface I was able to make copies of their storage without waking them. Somebody had thought to order them to dump their logs (which would void their warranties, but I guess since the facility was supposed to fall into the planet, nobody had cared). Unfortunately for that somebody, the diggers had dumped their logs into their buffers and then been shut down before the buffers timed out and deleted.

It was a lot of data, but I was able to construct a query to exclude the operation commands and other extraneous stuff. I had to make a direct connection to copy the data to the extra memory clips I'd implanted, which meant peeling back the skin around my right forearm weapon port again. Once I had that done, it went pretty quickly. I sat on the edge of the console, facing the door, and started up a favorite episode of *Rise and Fall of Sanctuary Moon* in background to help pass the time, though I kept one channel on Miki and the team feed.

I had just finished when Miki said, *Rin, is that you?*

I was distracted, stopping the episode, untangling myself from the console and from the sleeping, mostly empty brains of the diggers. I knew the team was still over in the hub for the bio pod (they were doing a physical assessment of the equipment for the bio matrices, and trying to get the consoles rebooted), so the question didn't make sense. *Is that me what?*

This. Miki sounded confused, worried. It sent me an audio clip. I heard the humans talking on the comms, Hirune and Ejiro, then Gerth made a comment.

The conversation? It was something about containment units not being where they were supposed to be, and I didn't understand why Miki was confused. *I'm still in the geo pod.*

No, Rin, this. Miki replayed the clip and stripped out the comms audio, so the human voices were much fainter. It was ambient audio, I could hear the air system. I could also hear light thumps, fast like a heartbeat . . . Oh, oh shit.

I wasted .002 seconds throwing a code into Miki's feed like I was responding to another SecUnit. I was at the hatch to the geo hub before I realized I needed to say it, or Miki wouldn't understand what to do. I slammed around the corner and up the corridor toward the lift junction. *Miki, you have an incoming unknown/potential hostile moving toward your position. Determine direction, then alert your clients, in that order.*

Miki widened its scan, and the rest of its senses went dark as it shifted all its attention to audio. It was rotating, trying to get a wider field. I was still getting the comms on the humans' feed, and Gerth said, "What's the little bot doing?"

"What's wrong, Miki?" Abene asked.

Rin— Miki stopped trying to sound like a human and sent me an urgent assistance request tied to the raw audio data. I should have realized, Miki wasn't a security bot, it had no code to deal with this and no one had ever shown it what to do in an emergency involving active and probably sentient hostiles. I reached the lift junction but the stupid lift had returned to a neutral station somewhere.

While I stood there like an idiot during the wasted seconds while the stupid lift returned to this position, I ran a quick analysis and compared it to the facility's schematic. I put markers up for Miki, the humans, and the incoming hostile, and shoved it back into Miki's feed. Miki was already saying, "Don Abene, something is coming toward us. We need to take the outer corridor back to the shuttle." It forwarded my active schematic to the humans.

I stepped into the lift as the doors opened. As I hit the destination sequence, I compared the ambient audio Miki was still processing with the projection on my schematic. This thing, whatever it was, was moving much faster than my first projection had indicated. I sent to Miki, *No time to withdraw, tell client to shelter in place and try to lock down area.*

Miki was saying to Abene, "Don Abene, it's too close, we have to stay here and seal the door."

But Wilken and Gerth had finally understood what was happening and I heard them shout at the assessment team to fall back down the corridor to the shuttle.

I didn't need to look at my projections again. They weren't going to make it to the end of the corridor. This is why humans shouldn't work security; the situation changes too fast and they can't keep up.

I had sent the lift to the bio pod, the nearest junction to the team's position. The door slid open and I stepped into a wall of sound: screaming, energy weapon fire. I ran down the corridor and rounded the corner.

I'm going to describe this as I reconstructed it from my and Miki's camera feeds later, since at the time even I was mostly thinking, *Oh shit oh shit.*

Wilken and Gerth had managed to get the group out of the bio hub, up the ramp, and into a junction with three other corridors, which was pretty much the most optimal point for being attacked in this area. I mean, if I was going to attack someone, I couldn't have picked a better spot.

I didn't have time to be too sarcastic about it because Wilken and Gerth were discharging their weapons down the corridor curving off to the left. Even the emergency power lights down there were off and I couldn't immediately see what they were shooting at. Ejiro was against the far wall, just sliding to the floor like something had slammed him aside. The rightward corridor led to the next segment of the bio pod and there was a lock and heavy hatch that was in the process of sliding closed. Miki, trying to follow my instructions, had triggered it via the emergency access on the wall. Brais staggered as if she'd been hit by something, and Abene grabbed her by the arm and steadied her.

It looked like all the humans were intact and Wilken and Gerth were driving off whatever it was they had blundered out here to meet and try to feed their clients to, and I was about to fall back. Then in the closing gap between the hatch and the wall, something moved. It was too fast for me to make it out without rerunning my video and reviewing it. Almost before I could move, it reached past Miki, grabbed Don Abene by the helmet, and yanked her into the gap.

Almost before I could move.

I crossed the junction toward them, ducked past Miki and Brais, hit the wall, used my momentum to go up two meters so I was level with Don Abene's body. I braced myself in the corner, planted one foot against the closing hatch and pushed. I felt the strain even in my inorganic parts; I couldn't keep it open for long.

One of Abene's flailing legs hit Brais and knocked her to the floor. Miki was the only one fast enough to act. It grabbed Don Abene's torso, and its whole feed was one scream of an urgent assistance code. I got an arm around Abene's waist, pinning one of her arms. The other was desperately scrabbling to hold onto Miki.

If she hadn't been wearing the suit, she would have been torn in half. If the hatch hadn't had a safety sensor that was giving us time to clear the obstruction, she would have been crushed. I wasted three seconds trying to pry at the spidery thing gripping her helmet. It was red and had eight multi-jointed fingers, that was all I could tell at the moment. Then I thought of the obvious solution. The air was breathable, and she could be treated for possible contamination as long as she still had her head.

I felt around her neck, slowed down by the unfamiliar suit design, then my fingers hit the little tab. (I would never have found it in time in my armor; the human skin overlay on my hands is much more sensitive.) I pressed the tab and twisted, and the emergency release unlocked her helmet. It was stuck in the door for almost a full second, enough time for me to push off and twist away. Then the thing on the other side snatched it out of the gap and the hatch snapped closed. I landed on my feet holding Don Abene, head still attached.

She slumped against me, gasping, her hands knotted in my jacket. Miki was at my shoulder, worriedly poking at her feed, its long fingers gently lifting her hair to check her neck. It said, "Don Abene, do you need medical assistance? Don Abene, please answer."

Gerth and Wilken stopped firing down the corridor, and my scan showed whatever was down there was long gone. From the floor, Brais gasped, "What was— Are you—" Ejiro, curled up at the base of the wall, shouted, "Abene!"

I was congratulating myself (because nobody else ever does it) on an excellent save. Human security had literally just noticed that something had tried to steal their client's head. Then Gerth said, "That's a SecUnit!"

All the humans stared at me and Abene. More importantly, Wilken and Gerth had pointed their weapons at me. Oh, Murderbot, what did you do?

(I don't even know. I suspect it has to do with the fact that I went from being told what to do and having every action monitored to being able to do whatever I wanted, and somewhere along the way my impulse control went to hell.)

The only way out of this was to kill them.

If I did that, I'd have to kill all of them. Including Miki. Including Abene. Her still-attached head was resting against my collarbone and her hair was all warm and soft where it was in contact with my human skin.

Right, so the only smart way out of this was to kill all of them. I was going to have to take the dumb way out of this.

I made sure my face and voice were SecUnit neutral. I said, "I'm a SecUnit under contract to Security Consultant Rin, who was sent by GoodNightLander Independent as an extra security measure for the assessment team."

I had to admit I was a SecUnit; there was no augmented human who could do what I just did. Also, my right sleeve was still rolled up, exposing the weapon port in my forearm. (The inorganic parts around the port might look like an augment designed to correct an injury, but the weapon port doesn't look like anything else but what it is.)

It was at this point I remembered Miki, and how I had told it I was an augmented human security consultant. I had been in Miki's feed, the connection so intimate even though I'd had my walls up. Miki would know that the Rin it had been talking to this whole time was the SecUnit standing here. Yeah, I should have taken Miki over earlier when I had the chance; there was no time to do it now.

In my private connection to Miki, I said, *Please, Miki, I just want to help.*

Miki cocked its head at me, then at Abene. Still dazed, and possibly concussed, she hadn't let go of me yet. She stared up at me, her brow wrinkled in confusion. Following my wounded human protocol, I had upped my body temperature to try to prevent her from going into shock. She said, "Miki . . . ? Who is this?"

Miki said, "Security Consultant Rin is my friend, Don Abene. I was asked not to tell you, to keep you safe."

Huh. That wasn't a lie, but it sure wasn't the truth, either. Maybe Miki had hidden depths.

I saw Gerth throw a startled glance at Wilken. Wilken

reacted but controlled it. They didn't speak on their feed connection. From the shuttle, Kader demanded an update, asking if the team needed assistance. Brais said, "Ejiro is injured." She pushed herself up the wall, shaking. "Is Abene all right? What happened?"

Abene started to nod, then winced. She patted my arm and pushed away a little, and I let her stand on her own. "I'm fine . . ." On the feed, she told Kader to hold his position. Aloud, she said, "Ejiro, how are you hurt?"

"It's my shoulder," Ejiro said. His voice indicated stress, his expression tense with pain. I started to tap MedSystem and remembered I didn't have one. (I know, I was all over the place.) Ejiro added, "What were those things? I couldn't see, just shapes."

Wilken and Gerth still aimed their weapons at me. Don Abene and Miki were blocking clear shots from this angle and if either Wilken or Gerth moved, I was going to have to do something about it.

Then Miki said, "Don Abene, Hirune is missing and is not answering her feed or comm."

Well, crap. They weren't my humans, I hadn't done a head count. I checked Hirune's feed, feeling Abene, Wilken, Gerth, Brais, and Ejiro all in there, too, calling for her. Her feed was still online, but it was inactive. That meant she was alive, but unconscious. I wasn't getting anything on my limited range scan, and neither was Miki.

On the comm from the shuttle, I heard Vibol cursing and Kader telling her to shut up and listen.

Abene's expression turned horrified. In the general feed, Miki replayed the last seconds before I got here. Breaking the images down, I saw a fast-moving shadowy shape approach from the main bio pod access corridor, just a sensor ghost in Miki's vision when Miki had hit the release to close the hatch. Then Miki had turned to go to the corridor that led toward the central facility, but was too late. All it had was a glimpse of the pinlights on Hirune's suit disappearing into the dark as she was dragged away, then Wilken and Gerth firing down the corridor after her. It had happened so fast, I don't think Wilken and Gerth had realized the hostile had taken Hirune.

As the humans reviewed the video in the team feed, Ejiro looked like he might be sick, and Brais swore softly. Abene turned to Gerth and Wilken. "We have to go after her. What were those things that— Why are you pointing that at me?"

They weren't pointing their weapons at her, but at me, just behind her. Wilken said, "That's a SecUnit, Don Abene, you need to step away from it until we sort this out. Where's this Rin? On the facility somewhere? It doesn't mesh with our brief from GI."

Abene had been in shock but I could practically see her brain slam back online. Her jaw set and her expression turned hard. She countered, "Where's Hirune? What took her? You're supposed to be our security."

Wilken held her ground. "Before we can look for her, I need to know why there's a SecUnit here. It's a fair question."

Miki sent into Abene's feed, *Please Don Abene, Rin is my friend. Please say you knew Rin was here.*

I thought there was no way Abene would take the word of her pet robot. (And granted, her pet robot was being loose with the facts, and phrasing the plea in a way that made it unclear that Consultant Rin and the SecUnit were actually the same, so its word wasn't worth much.)

Abene's angry gaze went from Wilken to Gerth. She said, "I didn't know Rin would be on the facility. GI informed me before we left. The oversight division was sending Rin to provide additional security—" She threw an opaque glance back at me. "Consultant Rin sent you?"

Fortunately I hadn't just been standing there like a moron and didn't drop the perfectly good opening she was trying to hand me. "I'm Consultant Rin's contracted SecUnit. Consultant Rin is on the station, and sent me to the facility on her shuttle."

Gerth said, "We weren't told about this." Wilken snapped a glare at her. Still no conversation between them on any private feed connection. There were a lot of questions they could ask. The scenario I had described, a client sending a

SecUnit out to provide security for another set of clients, was technically possible, but would violate bond company regulations and warranties. But Gerth took her weapon off me and pointed it where it should be, on the still-open corridor where the hostile had taken Hirune.

Abene snapped, "I don't care what you were told! We need to find Hirune! Brais, you have to get Ejiro back to the ship. Gerth, you go with them. Wilken, either help me or give me a gun and go back to the ship with the others." She switched to her feed to say, *Kader, inform the station PA of our situation. Tell them we're not sure what attacked us yet. Tell them to be wary of possible raiders in the system.* Kader acknowledged.

I can't help it, I like it when the humans are decisive. (Especially when it's the human who's in favor of not shooting me.) I said, "Consultant Rin has instructed me to help you in any way necessary." I kept my gaze on Abene because I was a SecUnit and that was what a SecUnit would do. You talk to the client and leave the people holding the guns to decide if they should feel threatened by what you said or not. (They should, they should feel really threatened.)

Wilken said hurriedly, "We're your security team, Don Abene, of course we'll go. But you should get back to the ship with Gerth and the others, and I'll go after Hirune with Rin's SecUnit."

Ejiro struggled to stand and Brais got under his good arm and levered him upright. Brais said, "I'm on the feed with Kader, Abene. Vibol's prepping the medical bay."

Since I was the SecUnit now and everything, I said, "Don't take a lift. The hostile may take control of the system and bring a lift to its position."

"I know that," Gerth snapped.

I know you know that, asshole.

Brais nodded at me and promised, "No lifts." She told Abene, "Please be careful."

Abene said, "You, too. Keep in contact with Kader." She turned to Wilken. "I don't have time to argue. We need to go."

Miki turned and started down the open corridor. Gerth had to step out of its way. Abene picked up her helmet and followed Miki. Wilken hesitated but gave Gerth a tap on the feed. Gerth motioned to Ejiro and Brais. "Come on, it'll be okay."

I waited until Wilken started after Abene, lengthening her stride to get in front. I moved up level with Abene, and backburnered Brais's feed so I could keep tabs on the group heading back to the shuttle.

Chapter Five

SOUNDING PROFESSIONALLY COMPETENT and not at all like someone who had just let a client get abducted, Wilken said, "My scan's not showing anything, but my range is limited. As long as Hirune's feed is still up, we can track her with it."

Really, you think? Miki had already set that up and informed Abene. I hadn't done anything yet but try not to panic.

I tapped my private channel to Miki and then had no idea what to say. ("Thank you for not exposing my lies" seemed a little too blatant.) Then Miki said, *You saved Don Abene, Rin/SecUnit.*

I had the feeling I needed to review my conversations with Miki and see where I went wrong. *Did you know I was a SecUnit, Miki?*

I don't know what being a SecUnit means. It's not included in my knowledge base. What should I call you if you're not Rin anymore?

Call me SecUnit. I had somehow committed myself to acting as a security consultant and I wasn't even going to get another hard currency card for it this time. As usual, I had no one to blame but myself. I thought it could turn out okay, though. All we had to do was retrieve Hirune, and then I'd think up a reason for why I needed a ride back on their shuttle, say I had to return to Consultant Rin, and then run off.

And possibly it could turn out better than okay. If GrayCris was behind the attack, then I could get video evidence of it to send back to Dr. Mensah along with my geo pod data.

The corridor was dark, and from her camera video Wilken was using her night-filter. Marker emergency lights on the floor and walls came on as we passed. Swearing softly, Abene tried to get her helmet back on, but I had broken the tab getting it off. She leaned down to leave it on the floor and asked Wilken, "Do you have any idea what attacked us? Some kind of bot? A retrieval device?"

That was a good guess, actually. I had one good image of the spidery hand thing, and I figured a comparison with the inventory of the bio pod would show it was something intended to work with or as part of a device designed to obtain surface samples. With the facility's system cores removed, there was no way to run that inventory. My theory was that the hostile that Miki had heard approaching had activated and used the retrieval device to distract the team while it grabbed Hirune. Wilken said, "My camera didn't pick it up. I believe raiders are in the facility and using the equipment left behind here against us. SecUnit, does Consultant Rin have any confirmation of that?"

I said, "Consultant Rin has no additional intel," because why should I do her work for her when I wasn't even getting a hard currency card, am I right?

On the feed, Abene asked Miki, *Miki, are you sure about this Consultant Rin? When did she contact you?*

On the station, Miki replied. *Rin is my friend. GI sent Rin to help you stay safe.* It added, *You were almost hurt, and Wilken and Gerth didn't try to help you at all.*

They were trying to protect Ejiro and Brais, Abene said absently, her mind obviously on something else, probably how terrible my cover story was. *There was no time.*

I didn't want her thinking about the likelihood of mysteriously appearing SecUnits and their (possibly apocryphal) security consultant contractors. I tapped her feed and said, *Don Abene, you can speak to me privately on this channel. I maintain contact with my clients at all times. Please note that Consultant Rin has specified that you are my principal client, not your security team.*

I was trying to let her know I was on her side, not theirs. I probably could have phrased it better. But I was pretty certain there were going to be sides, since Wilken and

Gerth clearly didn't believe it would be possible to recover Hirune.

That's the other problem with human security: they're allowed to give up.

Abene took a second to regroup, then asked me, *Do you know what took Hirune?*

I noted she had asked me again, directly, despite having heard the exchange with Wilken. Abene figured there were going to be sides, too. I said, *I think you're correct, I think it was a retrieval device. The hostile intended to take at least one member of the team and kill or injure others before retreating. That is not something a party of raiders would do.* I added, *Its plan is probably to draw you further into the facility to kill the rest of you, and hopefully cause more members of the team to leave the shuttle so it can kill them, too.* Trying to make things sound less dire than they are never helps. The client has to believe your assessment of the situation is accurate. (And I know, not my client.)

She took three seconds to process the fact that we were doing what the hostile probably wanted us to do. *But we have to find Hirune. Is there a way to counter it?*

You've already countered it. It doesn't know you have a SecUnit with you. For a human, that would be a hormone-fueled ego talking. For a SecUnit, it's just a fact. Like I told Tlacey before I killed her, I'm just telling you what I'm going to do.

Abene went quiet for five more seconds while we walked along the dark corridor. Then she asked, *Did you know there was something dangerous here? Did you know we would be attacked?*

I didn't know, not until Miki alerted me that something was approaching your position. That was true. I would much rather be hiding on the shuttle watching entertainment media right now. *Consultant Rin had no intel on hostiles inside the facility.*

Where were you? What did Rin really send you to do here?

I flailed mentally. Did I lie, did I tell the truth? It had to mesh with what I'd already told Miki, which was only partly a lie, sort of, and Abene might not register my hesitation but Miki would notice it unless I answered right now—*I was in the geo pod,* I said in desperation. *I was gathering data about a possible violation by GrayCris of the Strange Synthetics Accord.*

Ah, Don Abene said. *This begins to make sense.* She hesitated. *Can you save Hirune? If she's still alive.*

Yes. I'm pretty sure.

Abene let out her breath. *Good, then. We'll work together.*

Telling the truth was sort of working out for me.

We came out of the dark section into another corridor with low but active lighting. Wilken said, "Have you ever worked with a SecUnit before, Don Abene?"

"No. They're illegal in the homesystems." She was impatient. Right now she didn't want to hear anything from Wilken that didn't involve getting her friend back.

We were nearing a junction. Wilken signaled a halt through the feed, and paused while she took a scan. I was scanning continuously, but my readings were shit. The static had to be interference from the storm. Wilken continued, "I know you're close to your bot, but that thing is not like Miki. It's a killing machine."

Abene looked up at me and it was probably a mistake, but I looked down at her. It was surprisingly easy to make eye contact and not be nervous, maybe because I was used to seeing her face through Miki's feed. She touched her neck, the mark where the helmet rim had pressed in when the retrieval device had tried to wrench her head off. Her gaze went to Wilken's back again, but on our private channel she said, *I've never worked with a SecUnit before—I've never seen or interacted with a SecUnit before—so please tell me if you need any information or instruction from me.*

I had never had a human ask me how to give me orders before. It was an interesting novelty. *I have standing orders from Rin to assist you. I can do the rest.*

Wilken's scan picked up some interference, the same static at the edge of the range that both Miki and I were getting. We started to move again, taking the right-hand corridor leading away from the junction. Abene asked me, *Can you tell me why GI didn't inform me that there was a second assessment underway?*

I had an answer for this one and everything. *GrayCris has been accused of killing the members of a DeltFall survey team and attacking a PreservationAux team on a Corporation Rim assessment world. When you have access to newsfeeds again, check references to Port FreeCommerce for more information. There was reason to suspect GrayCris used this terraforming facility for interdicted activity and might try to prevent a reclamation effort.* That was all true, and it even sounded good when I said it.

I see. Abene sounded grim. *So GrayCris was using the facility to mine strange synthetics instead of to terraform, and they suspected a detailed survey of the remaining equipment would reveal it.*

Probably. I was certain of it, but it was longtime habit to give myself wiggle room if it turned out I was wrong. It didn't usually manage to prevent punishment from the governor module, but it was always worth a shot. *Until the geo pod data is reviewed and analyzed, we won't know for certain. Consultant Rin decided it was best to combine the data retrieval with additional security for your team.*

Ahead the corridor ended in an open space. Wilken signaled a halt, five seconds after I would have done it. The schematic said this was a transition zone between pods. The shadows ahead moved, but I could tell it was reflections from outside. There was a large view port to the left, like the one in the geo pod but in the wall, and the play of light and clouds cast shadows across the floor.

Wilken used her scan unit, then motioned us to move forward with her. The interference was worse but I was getting nothing on audio. I asked Miki, *Can you tell what's causing that scanner noise?*

No, SecUnit. I compared it to the static caused by the weather, and it looks the same, but it has a different source. That's strange, isn't it?

Wilken led the way into the large space, into the shadows from the storm churning on the other side of the transparent wall. Most of her attention was still on her scanner. Supports curved and twisted overhead, solid stationary metal somehow mimicking the constant motion of the cloud layers outside. There were three tall arched locks, open now to dark corridors leading off toward different pods. A gallery ran three quarters of the way around, opposite the transparent wall, with more corridor accesses. Miki's feed locater pointed toward the third corridor on the right on this level.

It's not strange, it's strategic, I told Miki. *Something is using the interference caused by the weather to mask a signal.* It was also frustrating. I missed having a SecSystem to do a real analysis. Even if we could break down the signal, I just didn't have the databases to match it to anything.

Miki switched to the general feed, *Don Abene, there is a signal using the storm interference to—*

I sensed motion, the whisper of sound as joints moved, and I flashed a warning to Miki just as a shape exploded off the gallery overhead. I caught Abene around the waist and bolted for that third corridor on the right, because that was the direction we needed to go to achieve our mission objective. Step one was to get there while the hostile was busy with Wilken.

I stopped far enough down the corridor to get Abene out of range of any stray friendly fire. (Wilken's weapon was discharging so rapidly I assumed she didn't have a lot of time to aim.)

Miki arrived a second later. I deposited Abene on her feet and she staggered before Miki caught her. Now this is something else I hate about human security. If Wilken was a SecUnit, my priority would be clear: continue ahead to retrieve Hirune, get her and Abene to safety, then return to retrieve/clean up what was left of Wilken and the hostile. But Wilken was human, so I had to go back and retrieve her stupid ass now.

Miki sent an image into my feed and said, *It's a combat bot!*

Yeah, thanks for the newsburst, Miki. I'd managed to get a clear picture of it while it was in mid-leap, when I was crossing the room with Abene. I told Miki, *Stay with Don Abene,* and ran back down the corridor.

Again, I know in the telling it sounds like I was on top of this situation but really, I was still just thinking, *Oh shit oh shit oh shit.* Combat bots are faster, stronger, and more heavily armed than me. Even if a SecSystem feed had been available, I couldn't hack a combat bot without making a direct physical connection, and trying for that would result in me being torn apart. (I've been torn apart before, and on my list of things to avoid, it was right up there at the top.)

The only good thing about combat bots is that they aren't combat SecUnits. Those are worse.

I exited the corridor at close to my top speed and had time to get one clear image of the situation to plot my attack. (I should put "plot" in quotes because it's really hard to plan under these circumstances.)

Wilken was on the floor and her large weapon had just been knocked out of her hands. The combat bot stooped over her. In shape it was close to a human-form bot. Sort of like Miki if Miki were three meters tall, had multiple weapon ports in its chest and back, four arms with multiple hand mods for cutting, slicing, delivering energy bursts, etc., and a not very endearing personality.

I went up the wall just enough to give myself the right trajectory, then pushed off into a jump and landed on the combat bot's head. Its cameras and scanners were up there, but the place where it did its actual processing and kept its memory was down in its lower abdomen. (So was Miki's; it was more protected down there since people always shoot for the head.) (At least, people always shot for my head, so I assumed they did it to bots, too.)

The combat bot knew I was a SecUnit because it sent a pulse through its skin that caused my pain sensors to max out. (I'd anticipated that and already dialed them down, but it didn't feel good.) The next pulse was meant to fry my armor and my explosive projectile weapon. Since I left both back at Port FreeCommerce, it didn't do much of anything to me and the mistake gave me the half second I needed to shove the port of the energy weapon in my right arm up against its sensory input collectors. I fired it at full capacity.

I had needed that half second, because just as I fired the bot swept its arm up and slammed me off its head. I hit the floor and slid three meters but the bot staggered sideways, temporarily (and I can't stress that "temporarily" part enough) blind, deaf, and with no ability to scan for movement or energy, no ability to acquire a target with any of its inbuilt weapons.

Wilken was just rolling over as I shoved upright. I

grabbed an explosive pack off her harness and threw myself at the combat bot. From the burst of static in the feed, it had just cleared its sensory inputs, but I'd already hit the spot just above its right hip joint and slammed the explosive pack into place.

It grabbed me by the head and shoulder, big hand gripping me, and I felt the shift in the metal that meant something sharp was about to come out of its hand. I thought, *Well, okay, that didn't work.* It could have destroyed me with any one of the many weapons in its chest, but it was mad and it wanted to make me hurt. Then there was a small muffled thump from the explosive pack.

The pack had two charges, and that was the first one, the one designed to bore a tunnel through heavy shielding and would do much the same to a combat bot's carapace. I still had the channel open to Wilken's feed and heard the pack's countdown start.

If the combat bot had been more self-aware, it might have stopped to crush my head, but its defensive mode kicked in and it shoved me away so it could get at the pack.

I hit the floor again and scrambled back as it clawed at the pack. Wilken rolled to her knees and opened fire at the bot's chest and head. She hit sensors and weapons ports, which granted, was a good idea. It was keeping the bot from targeting us while the charge had a chance to work.

The plastic outer casing came away but the explosive

had already tunneled through the bot's carapace. The bot tried to insert a probe into the hole to get the explosive. Wilken managed to hit the vulnerable joint as it extended. That bought the explosive the extra two seconds it needed. I put my hands over my head, tuned down my hearing, and rolled.

The explosion was muffled but I felt the vibration when the bot's body hit the floor. I came to my feet, mostly shocked that it had worked and that I was still alive and functional. (That's how SecUnits are taught to fight: throw your body at the target and kill the shit out of it, and hope they can fix you in a repair cubicle. Yes, I'm aware I didn't have armor or access to a repair cubicle anymore, very aware, but old habits die hard.)

The bot slumped on the floor like so much salvage. The carapace had contained the explosion, so there was no shrapnel, and the blast had damaged the bot's processor and the other important bits in its abdomen. But it was still active. I said to Wilken, "I need more packs."

She was sprawled on the floor, but her armor had protected her hearing. She yanked a set of packs off her harness and held them up.

I took them, armed each one, and dropped them into the bot's open carapace, then retreated.

Wilken staggered to her feet and backed away, covering the bot.

I reached the corridor entrance as the explosions went off. Each blast made the bot's body jerk and spasm. After the last one I scanned for activity. The bot still had power, but the charges had destroyed the first and secondary processors. That ought to do it.

Wilken was checking her scan. She made a relieved noise. "Good save. Come on. If there's one of those things here, there's more."

Well, yeah.

I followed Wilken up the corridor to where Miki and Abene waited. Abene had a hand on Miki's arm, holding on to it almost protectively. As we approached she let go and said, "Whoever activated that thing took Hirune, correct?"

"Has to be." Wilken tried to stop but Abene started up the corridor, and Wilken had to follow her. I got up in front, and Miki stayed beside Abene without prompting from me. Which was good; Miki might be no help in combat, but at least I knew Abene would be its priority, whatever Wilken told it to do.

I heard Abene in the feed for the shuttle, warning Vibol and the others and telling them again to stay onboard, not to come after us under any circumstances. Wilken sent her camera's recording of the attack to Gerth, and Gerth sent an acknowledgment. It was more professional than Kader, who was clearly agitated, but reported that they had sent a warning to the transit station and were keeping the PA updated.

Wilken added, "I've never seen raiders with access to combat bots, but there's a first time for everything."

I was pretty sure the combat bot had been original equipment for the facility. We were talking about GrayCris here, whose company motto seemed to be "profit by killing everybody and taking their stuff."

Abene didn't respond. After what I'd told her, she probably didn't think it was raiders, either. "They'll know we're coming."

They knew that already, I told her and Miki on our private three-way channel. And now the other combat bots would know a SecUnit was in play and adjust their strategy accordingly.

I wish I had a strategy.

[*Query: SecUnit active in watch zone.*]

I stopped. I did not scream, though I thought about it for .02 of a second.

I was pretty sure I kept my face blank, but Abene and Miki turned to look at me. Wilken kept moving.

I started to walk again, trying to figure out what channel it was coming in on so I could block it.

[*Query: respond.*]

In my feed, Miki said, *SecUnit, what is that?*

Don't answer it, Miki. It's a combat bot, trying to fix our position. Combat bots can't hack like combat SecUnits. They don't work linked to Sec or HubSystems like security SecUnits do. But still. I didn't want it in my head. Or Miki's head.

[*Query: SecUnit has subordinate unit.*] It sounded implacable, and amused. [*Query: pet bot.*]

I almost had it.

[*Objective: We will tear you apart.*]

I blocked the channel. I breathed out, slowly, so as not to draw attention from the humans. Miki sent me a glyph of distress. I said, *It's okay*, which was a complete lie. I reminded myself a combat bot wasn't a human, it wasn't a villain from one of my shows. It was a bot, and it wasn't threatening us.

It was just telling us what it was going to do.

Combat bots usually needed a human controller. Well, they needed a human controller when you were trying to achieve an objective. If the objective was as vague as *"attack everybody who lands on the facility while disguising your network feed traffic with static designed to match the interference created by the storm,"* maybe they didn't. But taking a prisoner, luring us further into the facility, did suggest a plan. GrayCris might have left an operative on the station, hiding out in plain sight with the Port Authority staff, keeping an eye on the facility. They had known when our shuttle left and when it docked with the facility, and had estimated how long it would take for the team to get into one of the pods and start the assessment. Then they sent a signal to activate the combat bots.

A signal that got through the facility's shielding? Maybe.

It would be nice to know how many bots, but at least now I knew the location of the first trap. It had failed, so the combat bots would be adjusting their position to create a second trap. I checked the schematic again, verifying that we were about to cross into the central hub.

I said, "Don Abene, I need to scout ahead. It'll be better if Wilken comes with me, and you and Miki wait here." I added on the feed, *And we need to hurry.*

Abene was all for hurrying and I didn't want to give Wilken time to argue. Abene said, "Yes, go ahead."

I started up the corridor, walking faster. Wilken hesitated, then followed me, her powered armor letting her catch up. "Hold it," she said. I stopped, to humor her, and because I could tell from the feed she was checking the schematic. "I see. Let's move."

I let Wilken lead the way.

We followed the tube that bypassed the central node to curve toward engineering. I'd been scanning automatically for drones, but I was still turning up a negative result. I tapped Miki's feed. *Have you checked the ship recently?*

I'm monitoring Kader's feed for Don Abene and checking the onboard system status every 2.4 seconds, SecUnit. Ejiro is in the medical suite and is expected to fully recover.

This was the first time I'd heard Miki sound even minimally annoyed. I was vaguely encouraged by that, for some reason. *Acknowledged, just checking.*

Miki sent me a smile glyph. *It's good to check on our friends.*

Well, I'd asked for that.

The tube curved ahead and, as I'd suspected, I saw the shadows and light play that indicated big windows in both walls. What we were about to do was an obvious tactic, and the combat bots could have sent some miniature drones up here to see if we tried it. But I wasn't picking up any hint of surveillance, movement, or suspicious static on my scan. It was support for the theory that they didn't have an on-site controller; the schematic didn't show that these access tubes had windows, it had just seemed likely given the rest of the facility's design. That wasn't something a combat bot was going to pick up on.

I stopped inside the shadow of the opaque part of the tube, and Wilken halted nearby. In the feed, I saw she was adjusting the magnification on her helmet cam.

One side of the transparent tube looked down at the engineering pod's hub. It was only twenty-two meters away at this point, and we had a view through the big curving roof, identical to the one in the geo pod. Wilken put her helmet cam against the tube wall, then sent me the video.

I could see the movement and extrapolate the positions myself, but the greater detail was nice.

One combat bot stalked across the hub floor as we watched, passing under a central sculptural structure that must have been part staircase to the upper gallery level, and part artistic statement. Wilken's scope registered powered movement in the upper level, and I could tell by the pattern it was a flight of combat drones. Most of my contracts used the much smaller (cheaper) model, designed for intel and better for collecting the clients' proprietary data, as well as keeping an eye on your base perimeter and making sure nothing snuck up on your teams in the field. These were the bigger model that had intel capacity, extra shielding, and an onboard energy weapon.

Still scanning, Wilken muttered, "So we've got one more combat bot, plus the drones."

We had at least two more combat bots; one was standing back under the shadow of the gallery. Wilken had missed it but I was extrapolating its existence based on the energy patterns Wilken's scope had picked up. I was willing to bet there were one or two more in reserve, or active somewhere else in the facility. Probably between us and the shuttle, because that's how these things work.

Then Wilken said, "There's the target."

By "target" she meant her client Hirune, lying on the floor next to the foot of the staircase. (You should never refer to the clients as targets; you don't want to get confused at the wrong moment.) (That's a joke.) She lay curled on her side, facing away from us, and I couldn't tell if she was alive. There was something else that worried me. "Why did they choose the engineering pod?"

We had to pass through the central node to get there, and unless there was a trap set there, the atmospheric pod was closer and better defended, as it only had the one entrance. The engineering pod had one access through the central node and a second tube branching off from the production pod, plus a lift junction in the hub, right under that gallery.

"No telling what goes on in bot brains," Wilken said, then threw a glance at me. I stared straight ahead. If there was one thing good about this situation, it was reinforcing how great my decisions to (a) hack my governor module and (b) escape were. Being a SecUnit sucked. I couldn't wait to get back to my wild rogue rampage of hitching rides on bot-piloted transports and watching my serials. Wilken added, "Let's go. I've got a plan."

Yeah, I've got a plan, too.

Now that we knew where the combat bots were, Wilken had us take the central node access to the production pod, where we could walk across the alternate tube access to the engineering pod. Or where I could walk across the alternate tube access, because that was her plan.

"We'll send the SecUnit in to distract them, and then I'll go in to get Hirune," Wilken told Abene.

Miki cocked its head. Abene's brow furrowed, and the look she threw at me was startled. "That's suicide, surely."

Wilken said patiently, "It's a SecUnit. That's what they do."

Miki signaled alarm through the feed. *This is not a good plan, SecUnit.*

Abene's expression went hard again. "It's against the GI standards of operation."

Wilken lifted her brows. "Do you want Hirune back?"

I watched Abene's face. She was struggling, torn between her fear for Hirune and the thought of sending me into what was probably going to be a terrible but at least abrupt death. It was interesting to watch, because she knew I was a SecUnit. She grated out, "There has to be another way. Consultant Rin would surely not allow this."

But she had said she had never seen or worked with a SecUnit before, and Miki didn't even have an entry in its knowledge base for it. And Abene was a human with a pet robot. She might think of me as Consultant's Rin pet, like Miki was hers.

We didn't have time to argue, and I really didn't want anybody thinking about Consultant Rin, whose fictional existence seemed to be increasingly flimsy, at least to me. I said, "It's all right, Don Abene. It's what I do." It was still extremely difficult not to sound ironic.

On our private connection, I said to her and Miki, *It's all right, I have another plan. It's safer for Hirune.*

Are you sure? Abene said, then, *You don't want to tell Wilken your plan.*

No, I didn't, mostly because I didn't want her giving me orders I had to ignore. Also because I had only a vague idea of what I wanted to do; most of it was going to be created on the fly. *You're my client. You can monitor me on this connection.* I told Wilken, "We should go now. Give me your weapon."

"What?" Wilken didn't fall back into a firing position, but the way the armor shifted over her joints made me think that was her first impulse.

I said, "If I'm going in first, I'll need a projectile weapon." I just wanted to see what she'd do.

"No, I'm going to follow you in," Wilken said, not so patiently. "I'll be at the hatch junction between the production pod corridor and the tube, to give you cover." She started up the corridor, telling Abene, "Wait here. If I send you a feed message to run, get back to the shuttle." I followed her, like a good little SecUnit/killing machine.

Behind me, Miki moved to watch us head away up the corridor, sending its camera-view to Abene.

Once we were out of earshot, Wilken muted her comm and feed and said, "Any word from Consultant Rin?"

"No, the station feed isn't accessible from here." Which Wilken knew. "I may be able to reach her on comm if you need to speak to her." I could fake that, but I'd need a little time to work on it.

Fortunately Wilken decided she didn't want to invite another Security Consultant to give opinions on her strategy, especially since she was planning on getting that Security Consultant's contracted SecUnit killed. I don't know what bond companies charge clients when we get killed, but it's probably a lot.

I figured Wilken's plan was to send me in, seal the hatch, and when the combat bots killed me, she would tell Abene and Miki that she had tried and now they needed to go back to the shuttle and leave. Without a SecUnit on her side, Abene was unarmed and not wearing powered armor, and Wilken could drag her back if Abene resisted. Of course, if Wilken touched Abene, Miki would intervene, but I'm not sure Wilken realized that.

We reached the hatch junction and Wilken stopped. She said, "Good luck."

Yeah, fuck you, I thought, and kept walking.

All right, so I wasn't happy about this. It wasn't like I had a repair cubicle waiting somewhere. I could repair with a MedSystem but I needed access to one, and the closest one I had any chance of getting to myself was onboard my cargo ship still docked at the station. But I knew I could do this.

(I hoped I could do this. I had been wondering a lot about my judgment lately.)

As I got further up the access tube, out of Wilken's sight, I backburnered her channel and tapped my connection to Miki and Abene to give them a visual through my feed. (It's not as good as a helmet camera would be; it uses my eyes to record so it jumps around a lot.) Miki was talking, more to Abene than to me, but I stopped listening. I was fishing for a drone.

I was broadcasting little spurts of static on an open channel. The drone should read it as signals from a vocal comm, like if some poor human was wandering through here, trying to call for help on their comm rather than on the secured interfaces Abene, Miki, and Wilken were using for our feed.

This could blow up in my face in that all the drones might decide to slam through here at once to get me, but I didn't think that would happen. The bots hadn't sent them after us yet because they didn't want us to know they had them, probably because that's how they intended to attack the shuttle. I was hoping the drones were set to protect the perimeter and a sentry would come to investigate.

I came to a spot where a connector in the tube had empty slots where equipment was supposed to be fitted. It formed shadowy cubbies and I stepped into one. My scan stretched as far as it would go, still sending my tempting intermittent signal. And I got a response. A staticky burst, like a comm trying to reply to me and being drowned out by interference.

A normal SecUnit (you know, one that still had its governor module, less anxious than me but probably more depressed) could do this part, but would be restricted to the canned responses available in the combat stealth module. A drone might be able to recognize those responses as coming from another combat unit and not a human. I didn't have the combat stealth module anyway (I had never been upgraded with it, probably due to RaviHyral and the whole "killing all the clients" thing, go figure), so I used snippets of dialog from my media storage, extracted and processed to eliminate background noise and music and to remove any identifying code underlying the audio. I sent my prerecorded "Are you—can't find—where—ship—" artistically obscured with static.

The drone sent another artistic burst of static in response. From its signal strength it was getting closer. I stayed where I was, waiting.

On the feed, Miki said, *We're worried about what you're doing, SecUnit.*

Nothing on scan yet, so I had time to chat. *Why are you worried, Miki?*

Because we don't know what you're doing. Wilken is telling Dr. Abene on her feed that you aren't doing anything—

The drone had just come into my scan range, moving slowly so as not to alert the human it thought was here. Standing in the dark cubby, I had stopped breathing, stopped any activity it might pick up. I teased it with a little more comm audio. The schematic showed these slots as part of an atmospheric gas sampling station, so the drone had no idea there was room for something human-sized to hide. Confused at the apparently empty passage, it tried to trace the signal. And I pinged it with a compressed list of drone control keys.

(That's not in the stealth module, and it's not a function of company-supplied SecSystems. I got it from the proprietary data of a company client who worked on countermeasures for combat drones. I had managed to resist deleting it to fill that space up with new serials. I knew someday it would come in handy.)

One of the keys worked and the drone switched into neutral standby. I wandered around in its control code for a minute or two, making sure I knew how it worked. It, all the other drones (it was reading thirty active), and three combat bots were all operating on a secured feed. All the drones were in the engineering pod foyer with two of the combat bots. The third bot was reading as active in the facility, but there was no location for it. (I had a bad feeling it was heading toward the shuttle to cut us off.) The bots had more layers of security and even now, from within their own network, if I started trying to hack them they'd have time to run up here and kill me. But I could take control of all the drones.

In another twenty seconds, they were all my new drone friends.

Oh, I see, Miki said. *Never mind.*

But I was going to have to move fast. I told Drone One to remain in standby, and ordered the twenty-nine others to turn on the two combat bots in the engineering pod. Then I started to run.

I rounded a curve, went through two open hatch junctions. I was already hearing energy and projectile weapon fire, metal smashing against walls, and that funny high-pitched whine combat drones make when attacked. I wasn't controlling them individually; once given the order, the drones knew what to do, and me trying to jump-seat pilot them would just slow them down.

I accelerated as the hatch entrance to the engineering pod came into sight. I reached the end of the corridor at top speed and threw myself forward into a dive.

The hub foyer was now a warzone. I hit the floor and slid out across it. The combat bot nearest the door flailed wildly at the cloud of drones firing and diving at it. It thrashed around like an irritated metal whirlwind, stray blasts from its weapons hitting the walls, the floor, the columns. It smacked a drone with its cutting hand and shrapnel sprayed the room. I'd tuned down my pain sensors in anticipation, but I still felt impacts all over my back and shoulders, little thumps that I knew meant something had cut through my clothes and pierced my skin. (Does that sound terrifying? Because it was terrifying.) The second bot tried to run forward but the drones made a wall and slammed into it, forcing it back with a haze of weapon fire and their own armored bodies.

I rolled to my feet, dove again, and landed next to Hirune. Her body looked intact and I didn't see any blood pools, but I didn't have time to check if she was alive. (It didn't matter. In a retrieval like this, humans wouldn't believe the hostage was dead unless I brought the body back.) I scooped her up and here came the hard part, I had to run out of the foyer.

The bots had had time to figure out (a) the SecUnit was here (b) what the SecUnit had done to take over their drones and consequently (c) they were really pissed off at that SecUnit. I bolted across the room toward the door.

The two bots had taken out twenty-three of the drones, each one a light, a connection, blinking out of my awareness. But the drones had done a lot of damage, targeting joints, weapons ports, and hands. A camera view from a surviving drone told me the bot behind me had lunged for my retreating back but crashed to its knees; drones had been concentrating fire on its ankle joints while others distracted it.

The bot in front of me threw itself forward to block the door. And I turned right and ran straight for the lift junction.

The combat bots had taken over the lift system like I'd warned Brais, but combat bots can't hack like a SecUnit. I hadn't tried for control of the whole system, just this one lift, telling it to wait here for me. The door slid obediently open as I reached it. I ordered it to take me to the production pod. The door slammed on a set of sharp metal fingers and the pod whisked me away.

Drone One was still waiting in the corridor, and I

ordered it to close the junction hatches between the engineering pod and the production pod, drill through the walls, and fuse the controls. It whizzed into action as the lift stopped and opened its doors.

I stepped out into an empty junction in the production pod, and sent the code I'd prepared into the lift system. It shut the system down and set a password lock. The combat bots could get past it if they had the right code modules, and if they devoted resources to it that they could be using for other things. It would still buy me the time I needed. I hoped.

Now that I had time to evaluate my own condition, I eased up my pain sensors a little. The impacts I'd felt turned from dull aches to sharp burning, like little explosions under my skin. Ow, ow, okay, ow. I locked my knee joints to stay upright and upped my air intake.

I had taken multiple shrapnel hits from the drones being shredded all around me. I had two hits from projectile weapons, one in my lower left side and one in my left shoulder. I was pretty certain I had been hit by stray shots meant for drones. If the bots had been able to target me, I would be in pieces. I tuned down my pain sensors and the impact sites faded from explosions down to embers. (I know that's actually not a permanent solution and pretending bad things aren't happening is not a great survival strategy in the long run, but there was nothing I could do about it now.) The arm where I was storing my memory clips was undamaged, which was a relief.

I started down the corridor toward the production pod foyer, where the others should be.

I tapped Miki's feed for a report because neither it nor Abene were saying anything and I wasn't sure what they had been able to see through my visual feed. At that point, Hirune's gloved hand squeezed my shoulder.

Fortunately I remembered I was carrying a possibly living human and didn't scream or drop her or anything. Her helmet with its comm mic had been ripped off, and her head rested on my shoulder. She slurred the words, "Who are you?"

I was distracted, and what came out of my buffer was the standard, "I'm your contracted SecUnit." I was distracted because confused noise was coming from the connection with Miki and Abene. It wasn't communication from a feed interface, it was audio; Miki was sending me open comm audio over the feed.

Her voice rough and deep with fury, Abene shouted, "Who sent you? GrayCris?"

On my shoulder, Hirune made a confused "huh?" sound.

The other comm audio I could hear was too faint even for me to tell what it was. I had to waste four seconds converting it to a spectrogram before I recognized it. It was two noises, the low pitch of Miki's joints and the higher pitch of powered armor, bracing against each other.

Well, shit.

I do make mistakes (I keep a running tally in a special file) and it looked like I had made a big one. I had interpreted all of Wilken's behavior as being about me, about the discomfort and paranoia associated with a SecUnit suddenly appearing out of nowhere, supposedly sent by another security consultant whose existence implied that the clients didn't trust her and Gerth. (I know, the "it's all about me" bit is usually a human thing.) But now it seemed she had been uneasy for a whole other reason.

The good thing about getting your security through a bond company like the one that had owned me is that for small contracts you take delivery at a company office, and for big ones it arrives in a company transport. This greatly reduces opportunities for somebody to show up pretending to be your security team when they've really been contracted to kill you.

Wilken and Gerth were good. I had listened in on and analyzed their conversations aboard Ship and not picked up any hint of it. But then, if they worked for GrayCris, they would be alert for the kind of bond company security surveillance in use throughout the Corporation Rim.

By this point my drone had reached the hatch junction where Wilken was supposed to be waiting. She wasn't there, obviously, being busy betraying her clients. (When I said I didn't like humans working security you thought I was just being an asshole, right?)

I used my connection to Miki's feed and accessed its camera view. Oh yeah, not good. The image was shaky but I could see Miki had Wilken backed up against a pillar. Miki had one arm pinning Wilken's right wrist against the pillar, as Wilken tried to bring her projectile weapon down to bear on Abene. Something was wrong with Miki's hand but I didn't have a clear view, and I didn't want to distract Miki at the moment by pulling a damage report. Wilken had her other forearm braced against Miki's face, like she was trying to shove it away, but that wasn't what she was doing. She had energy weapons built into the forearms of her armor and she was trying to slide one into position to blow Miki's head off.

(Miki could operate without its head, but its sensory inputs and cameras were there, and it would be really awkward.)

Wilken had cut me out of her feed connection, but I used Abene's to bypass the block: *This is SecUnit. We can talk about this. Consultant Rin can offer you immunity from prosecution if you testify.* I hoped that made sense (it was a line from *Sanctuary Moon*) and I'm sure it sounded like I was stalling. I wasn't stalling and I didn't need her to answer me, I just needed her distracted enough to not think about what I was doing in her feed. *Your bosses are going down. Whatever they paid you, it won't make up for a stint in prison.* (Yeah, that was from *Sanctuary Moon*, too.) In the meantime, I was frantically looking for the right code. The companies that make powered armor are different from the ones that make SecSystems, intel drones, cameras, and so on, and their system architectures were different and it made everything harder.

Abene had a grip on Wilken's projectile weapon, trying to help Miki wrench it away, but couldn't do much against the powered armor. I could tell she had no idea about the forearm energy weapon, which was in a much more dangerous position. In the feed, I could hear Abene telling Miki to let go and run, and Miki refusing on the basis that Wilken would then shoot Abene. Who should be running, frankly, but wasn't going without Miki, obviously.

I reached the turn into the production pod's foyer where Abene and Miki struggled with Wilken. Her energy weapon slid slowly but inexorably into position next to Miki's head, despite its attempts to hold her and Abene hanging off her other arm and kicking her. In about thirty seconds I was going to have to put Hirune down on the floor and do this the hard way, if I couldn't find this code.

On yet another channel, Drone One reported that it couldn't detect any activity suggesting that the combat bots were trying to blast their way through the hatches it had sealed and jammed. The drone had been cut off from the network and couldn't report further on the movements of any active units. Which meant that the combat bots had stopped to repair each other (Yes, they're self-repairing unless their main processing center is destroyed. Yes, that is a pain in the ass and also terrifying.) and would soon be taking another route out of the engineering pod to come after us. Like I didn't have enough to do right now.

Frantically scanning Wilken's armor, I finally found the right code. That was a relief. I opened a channel and sent the "freeze" command via the feed.

The reason the company doesn't use powered armor like Wilken's is not only because the company is cheap. Powered armor like Wilken's is hackable.

Miki twisted free and stepped backward, still keeping its body between Wilken and Abene. Wilken froze in place (literally) her face grimacing as she shouted into a comm that wasn't working anymore. (I had cut off her comm and feed; I wanted current developments to be a surprise to Gerth.) The projectile weapon started to fall from Wilken's frozen fingers and Abene lunged forward and grabbed it.

Now I could see Miki's damage; it had two energy impacts on its chestplate and its right hand was a stump.

I said, "It's all right, I've locked her armor." I ran Miki's feed back, skimming it to see what had happened. Wilken had waited until I was busy with the combat bots, then had returned to Abene and Miki. She had moved toward them fast, saying she had something important to tell them off the comm and feed. Then she had grabbed Abene by her hair. It was still hanging loose, her helmet left behind after I'd broken the release tab to get her away from the bio sampler.

Wilken had pointed the weapon at Abene's head and said, "Sorry, it's not personal." That comment had cost her the kill, it had given Miki time to slam in between them and force the weapon up and away. (Just because Miki was a pet bot that carried things for humans didn't mean it wasn't strong enough to take on powered armor.) Wilken had fired the weapon, destroying Miki's hand, which hadn't slowed Miki down, either.

Abene saw me and gasped, "Hirune—"

"She's alive," I said, because Abene was armed now and traumatized humans with unsecured weapons make me nervous.

Miki said plaintively, "SecUnit, Consultant Wilken tried to shoot Don Abene."

Abene slung the weapon over her shoulder and hurried to me. She touched Hirune's face, then looked up at me. "Oh thank you, thank you."

It's nice to be thanked. "Miki, damage report."

"I am at eighty-six percent functional capacity." It held up its arm stump. "It's only a flesh wound."

For fuck's sake. Abene turned toward it, shocked. "Miki, your poor hand!"

Oh good, another Abene/Miki lovefest. I said, "Miki, take Hirune."

Miki stepped forward and held out its arms. Hirune was only semiconscious but had a convulsive grip on my jacket. Abene gently pried her hand away and I deposited her into Miki's arms.

I turned to Wilken. It was the hair-grabbing thing that bothered me. Along with the snide "it's not personal." If Wilken had shot with no warning, Abene would be dead and Miki would be in pieces now. But Wilken had wanted Abene to know that she was betrayed. That was personal.

I don't like personal.

This was another reason I didn't like human security consultants. Some of them enjoyed their job too much.

I stepped up to Wilken and pulled off the utility harness that held the explosive packs and other gear. She glared at me through the faceplate. I slung the harness over my shoulder and said, "Don Abene, you might not want to watch this."

Abene turned away from Miki and Hirune. "No!" Then she added more calmly, "I know you're angry that she sent you to the combat bots, but don't kill her."

I wasn't angry on my account. Being sent into situations to get shot at was literally my job, or had been my job. I thought everything had happened so fast Abene hadn't had time to process what Wilken had nearly done to her.

It must have been obvious that her first argument was not compelling, because Abene continued, "If she's working for GrayCris, we need her as a witness."

Okay, that did make sense. The whole reason I was here was to find more evidence against GrayCris. I looked into Wilken's faceplate. Her expression had gone blank, trying to conceal fear. With her comm and feed down, she could still hear us, though our voices would sound like we were at the bottom of a mining tunnel. When it powered down, the armor had automatically opened some vents to allow air circulation, so she wouldn't suffocate or cook in her own heat. I could give it a delayed command to close the vents once we'd left, and Abene would think it was an accident.

There's that caring thing again. Did I care if Wilken survived or not? Not really.

I said, "We need to go," and held out my hand for Wilken's projectile weapon. Abene handed it to me, and I walked away. I left the vents open.

As Miki and Abene followed me, I said, "The bots in the engineering pod will be trying to reach us once they self-repair, and the drone I captured says that there's one more active combat bot. It's probably somewhere between us and the shuttle." We also knew they would use whatever mobile equipment was left behind in the facility against us. I didn't want to have to fight another bio sampler.

Abene lengthened her stride to keep up with me. "I can't reach the shuttle on my feed or comm," she said. "Neither can Miki."

"That's because I'm blocking you," I told her. "I didn't want you to say anything that might alert Gerth." At least not until I figured out what to do about Gerth. I couldn't get to her armor from here, even if I unblocked the feed. The codes for the armor were unique to each unit (the manufacturers weren't completely stupid) so I had to be close enough to be able to scan for them.

"I see." Abene, amazingly, didn't argue. Or maybe it wasn't amazingly; she was pretty smart. "I suppose it's too much to hope that Gerth is not also a hired killer."

"Analysis from the cargo ship suggested they had worked together for some time," I said. "We have to assume they were suborned together, or at some point deflected and replaced the security team your company sent."

"Deflected," Abene repeated. "That means killed?"

"Probably." When I picked up the Milu cargo ship on

HaveRatton, I hadn't downloaded any local news, just the bursts about Port FreeCommerce and GrayCris. If there had been reports of two bodies discovered with all identification burned out, I had missed them. (You can't space people off a transit ring; security looks for that kind of thing and gets very agitated about it.) "With Gerth at the ship, we have a hostage situation."

I hate hostage situations. Even when I'm the one with the hostages.

Miki said, "That's not good."

See, that? That is just annoying. That contributed nothing to the conversation and was just a pointless vocalization to make the humans comfortable.

In her feed, Abene was doing a quick review of my video from the engineering pod. It was less than a minute, so it didn't take her long. She said, "Was Wilken giving the bots orders? Perhaps they will go dormant without her. But if they report to Gerth, we're back in the same situation."

"I don't think she or Gerth gave them orders," I said. "I was listening in on their feeds, and I would have heard that, even if it was encrypted." They hadn't spoken to each other much at all, which was maybe suspicious in itself. (I know, hindsight is awesome.)

Miki said, "The combat bots could have been in standby and received instructions to activate once anyone arrived at the facility." Hirune stirred and murmured and Miki responded, "There, there, Hirune. It's all right."

Well, yeah, I thought of that already.

Abene was saying, "I don't understand this. If Wilken and Gerth were sent to kill us, why were the combat bots sent here? Obviously GrayCris wants to stop the assessment, but that's—"

I said, "Hold it," and stopped. I needed to do a quick review of my video and prove or disprove this theory and there's only so many things I can do while walking and scanning for hostiles without a Sec- or HubSystem to help. I let Miki view my feed as I started my analysis, and I was distantly aware of Miki explaining to Abene what I was doing.

I pinged my drone and told it to open its log and query its records and build a list of activations, standbys, and sleep phases. Then I pulled my copy of Miki's video of the first attack when Hirune had been taken, and did a quick review of it and my video of the second attack, when the combat bot had gone after Wilken. I finished and then checked the log digest the drone had ready for me. (It was really nice to work with such an advanced drone.)

"The combat bots and drones weren't sent here for you," I reported to Abene. "They were part of the facility's manifest from the start. The transit station was still in construction at that point, and wouldn't have been much help in driving off potential raiders. And GrayCris wouldn't have wanted to call on any outside agency for help, since they were trying to conceal the fact that they were building an illegal mining platform disguised as a terraforming facility." And the bots probably weren't here just for protection from raiders, but also to keep any human workers in line. "The combat bots and drones have been in sleep mode since the facility was abandoned. They were activated when your shuttle docked here. Analysis suggests Wilken and Gerth were surprised by their existence." A bot analysis would have missed that entirely, but I'm better at reading human faces and voices. (The organic parts in my head do come in handy for that, and of course it was much easier on recorded video, when I could do freezes and zoom-ins, and not in anxiety-causing realtime.) "I think Wilken did believe it was raiders who staged the attack and took Hirune, up until the second attack when she saw the combat bot. There's a good chance GrayCris didn't tell her and Gerth about the combat bots, hoping that the bots would eliminate them." And helpfully tie up any loose ends.

I wondered how Wilken felt about that. It sure hadn't made her hesitate to finish her mission. She had expected me to be destroyed by the combat bots; she meant to kill Abene and Miki. She had counted on getting out of this and collecting her fee.

Abene let out a breath in frustration and anger. But she said, "Can we use that on Gerth, do you think? Tell her that GrayCris tried to kill her and Wilken as well, that they should testify to what happened. Or use Wilken as a hostage ..." She shook her head, biting her lip.

She was thinking strategically, which is always a relief, and asking me questions instead of giving me stupid orders. I didn't have to obey orders anymore, but that doesn't make them any less annoying. I said, "Our only advantage right now is that Gerth doesn't know Wilken was compromised."

The drone was still reporting no activity from the hatches, which meant the bots had gone the other direction, or were working on the lifts. I told it to come to my position. (When it reached Wilken, I had it stop and hover in front of her face for twenty-six seconds. Okay, so I was a little angry.)

Abene was looking at me again. I could see her doing it from the view through Miki's camera. She said, "Gerth must be waiting for a sign from Wilken before she acts against the others on the shuttle, surely. I should try to contact Kader. I can get a tight feed connection with him."

"Are you sure he won't say aloud, 'Hey everybody, Don Abene's just signaled me on the feed' before you can tell him not to?" That's a problem with humans.

Abene started to speak, hesitated, and then shook her head once. "He might, he might. But we must find out what is happening aboard the shuttle."

Miki said, "Vibol doesn't speak very fast. Maybe we should call her."

I sent Abene and Miki a warning in the feed right before the drone passed us in silent mode; I was sending it ahead to scout. Abene still flinched, then stared after it. But she was right about the shuttle. If we could get a report from onboard, it would help us plan. Also, Abene and Miki would stop asking me about it, which would be a very big bonus right now. (I'd forgotten how stressful being a SecUnit was.) I said, "You don't have any security monitoring aboard your shuttle? No cameras? No other bots, even a currently inactive one?"

"No." Abene pushed her hair back, frustrated but thinking. "There's no need. There are cameras in the evac suit helmets, but they're inactive in the emergency lockers."

Miki said, "Don Abene, there are two evac suits on the flight deck. I have the hard addresses for their comms."

Abene turned to me. "Can you activate their comms from here?"

I probably could. But whether Gerth had killed the others yet, or was still waiting for a signal from Wilken, it didn't matter. We still needed to get Gerth off the shuttle.

We needed to get everyone off the shuttle.

I was getting an idea. It was probably a bad idea. (When most of your training in tactical thinking comes from adventure shows, that does tend to happen.) I said, "We need to get back to the geo pod."

Chapter Six

NOW THAT I KNEW where we were going, it was a lot easier to get there. We went to the next lift junction, and I spent a careful minute cutting my code-protected lift out of the system and making its actions invisible to the rest of the lifts. (That sounds like an obvious thing to do, but the problem is, if the other lifts can't see your lift, they can attempt to occupy the space your lift is already in. This is just as catastrophic for the occupants as it sounds.)

I sent my drone on the lift first, just to make sure there was nobody waiting for us outside the geo pod, then I took Miki, Abene, and Hirune through. We reached the geo pod hub, walking in under the transparent dome with the shifting storm clouds overhead. I sealed and code-locked the hatches, which admittedly was just to make the humans feel better. The combat bots could blast their way through if they tried hard enough, especially with three of them concentrating on one hatch. I was hoping they were planning to trap us on the route to the shuttle, which was not a great scenario either, but would at least buy us some time. I sent the drone to scout the access corridors that led to the shuttle to see if it could locate the bots' ambush point.

(I didn't think the bots would use the lifts even if they got control of the system again, since they would be alert for the kinds of things SecUnits can do. But I told my invisible lift pod to careen randomly around the facility anyway. It was worth a shot.)

Anyway, Step One to getting us back in the shuttle was getting Gerth out of it.

It occurred to me I could do this faster if I had help. Miki had put a semi-conscious Hirune down in one of the padded console chairs while Abene pulled the emergency kit off her harness and rifled through it. I said, "I'm going to try to get a feed connection to your shuttle via the suit comms on the flight deck, but I need to get this control station active. There are diggers still attached to the facility that we might be able to use against the combat bots." That wasn't exactly what I was going to do with the diggers, but I didn't want to argue about it.

Abene nodded understanding and put the med tabs for concussion and shock into Miki's good hand. "Miki, please take care of Hirune while I work on the control station." Then she frowned at me and said, "You're bleeding."

I looked down. I was dripping onto the floor, a mix of blood and fluid. I hate it when I leak. My veins seal automatically and some of the shrapnel had popped out, but the projectile in my side had moved around, reopening that wound. I cautiously dialed up my pain sensors to check; oh yeah, that's what had happened. Ouch.

Abene said, "Were you hit?" She stepped toward me, reaching to push my jacket aside.

I jerked back a step. She stopped, startled. Miki turned, its visual sensors focusing in on me. I checked its camera and got a view of my face. I thought I had gotten good at controlling my expression, but apparently only when I wasn't feeling actual emotions. In our feed connection, Miki said, *Abene won't hurt you, SecUnit.*

Abene held up her empty hand, palm out in a gesture that usually meant "don't shoot me," except she wasn't afraid. She was matter-of-fact. She said, "I'm sorry, but you need treatment. Will it be better if Miki helps you?"

I said, "I don't—" and stopped there because I didn't have any way to finish that sentence. I needed help, I didn't want anyone to touch me. These were two mutually exclusive states.

Abene waited, watching me. Then she said, "Miki, can you leave Hirune?"

"I'm okay," Hirune rasped. She was blinking and clutching a bulb of hydrating solution from the emergency kit. "I'm fine."

Abene said, "Good. I'll work on the console and Miki,

you come here and help Rin." Still watching me, she held out the emergency kit and Miki came to take it.

As Abene went to the console, Miki said, "Please lift your left arm and pull your shirt up, SecUnit."

I had to set down Wilken's projectile weapon and harness to do that. I did, putting them on the station chair behind me, because it would look like a normal SecUnit thing to do, because I needed to look normal now. I was devoting a lot of attention to the response I needed to make to Abene. I decided a simple error correcting statement was best. "I'm not Rin. Rin is—"

Abene was powering up the digger control station. Not looking at me, studying the console's interface in the feed, she said, "Consultant Rin is your supervisor, yes, I'm sorry."

Miki scanned me and sent the results to my feed. Wow, those were kind of big chunks of metal stuck in me. Miki extended a secondary clamp out of its chest and used that to hold the emergency kit as it got the extractor probe out with its good hand. *I don't need the nerve-block,* I told Miki on the feed. *I can turn my pain sensors down.*

That must be handy. Miki poked the probe into the wound in my side. *I don't have pain sensors, but then, I don't have pain.*

Yeah, one of the differences between bots and SecUnits. I had talked to ART about the other differences, once. How we couldn't trust each other, because of the orders humans could give. And ART had said, *There are no humans here.*

Well, there were humans here. I said, *Miki, did you tell Don Abene that there is no Consultant Rin, there's just me?*

Yes, Miki said. It found the projectile and carefully eased it out. *I told her when the first combat bot attacked Wilken, when she asked me if I knew if you were telling the truth.* Then it added, *I told her because I wanted to, not because I had to.*

I was sure Miki believed that. *Why does she think I lied about it?*

She thinks it's because it's illegal in the jurisdictions that GoodNightLander Independent operates in to employ Sec-Units. Miki finished applying the wound sealant patch and went for the second projectile. *She said someone who works for GoodNightLander Independent must have sent you here but doesn't want us to know who they are. She said it didn't matter, since they sent you to help us.*

Abene was using the console to boot the interfaces for each digger. I needed to start trying to get intel on the shuttle.

It was tricky since I wanted to keep Abene and Miki's comm and feed connections cut off so Gerth or anything else that might be wandering the facility with murderous intent couldn't use them to trace us. But it helped that

Miki had the hard addresses for the two suits on the flight deck. The shuttle's feed was still active, and I was able to sneak in and ping the first suit. After some poking, I got it to activate its comm.

I heard Kader first, asking for a report on Ejiro's condition. Brais answered, saying the MedSystem had put Ejiro into recovery. Vibol said something in the background that the audio couldn't quite pick up. Then I heard Gerth say, "Any response from the station yet?"

Sounding frustrated, Kader replied, "Not yet. It's got to be interference from that storm."

Vibol spoke again, still too muffled. Gerth answered, "No, we need to sit tight until we hear from them."

Uh-huh. She sounded calm and confident and reassuring, though I was pretty sure a voice analysis would show the tension underneath.

I pulled out of the connection and backburnered it. Abene had the station display set to visible, floating above the console's surface, showing the control screens for the diggers. She muttered, "There. All the diggers are powering up. It's going to take a few minutes. I hope you can control them, it looks like their procedures have all been deleted."

Miki was picking shrapnel out of my back now. I said, "The rest of the team hasn't been injured and Gerth is still acting as their security. She won't let them leave the shuttle to look for you. They're having trouble contacting the station for help."

Abene looked up, frowning. "What trouble? We were in contact with the station when we arrived. It shouldn't—"

I actually lost the rest of it because my drone pinged me with a report. It had reached the decontam room and had the hatch of the shuttle in scan range, and it hadn't found any sign of the combat bots. I said aloud, "They aren't there."

"What?" Abene stood up from the console, alarmed. "Who?"

"The combat bots. The drone didn't find them on the route to the shuttle." I was skimming through everything it was sending me, the scans, the visual data, audio. The drone's scan was a lot better than mine, and it had been actively searching the route, checking spots for potential ambush. Comparing it to the schematic, I couldn't see anything it had missed. "They aren't there." I sent the drone's visual into our closed feed connection.

Miki's head cocked as it reviewed the video. Abene threw a worried look at Hirune. She said, "Then they must be here, near this pod, trying to trap us."

Maybe. I found my careening invisible lift pod, told it to go to the nearest lift junction to the drone, and ordered the drone to take the lift to the junction outside the geo pod. Within a minute the drone was in the access corridors outside the hatches I had sealed, scanning. I watched it record empty corridors and junctions. Nothing. The bots weren't setting up an ambush for us on the way to the shuttle and they weren't outside the geo pod.

My potential strategy hadn't experienced a catastrophic failure or anything, but I was missing something.

Right, this wasn't a good time to panic. I went back to my first contact with the drone, the intel I'd gotten before it had been locked out of the combat bots' network. There was the entry for that third active combat bot. It was marked "active out of range."

I had assumed it was out of range because it was headed toward where the shuttle was docked, to set up a trap for us when we tried to retreat, but I didn't know that.

Go back further. Wilken and Gerth had been sent here in place of the contracted GI security to stop/kill the assessment team. So why hadn't they acted as soon as they arrived on the transit station? With so few people there, it wouldn't have been difficult. They would have needed an exit scenario if they had acted on the station, but they needed an exit scenario even more here on the facility. The team's shuttle wasn't wormhole capable. They would have to return to the transit station, kill the PA staff who would possibly be asking a lot of questions about what had happened to the rest of the assessment team, and steal a wormhole capable ship. (Preferably a ship without a bot pilot who would vigorously resist being stolen.) That sounded like a lot of work, especially considering the fact that there were combat bots on the facility, ready to destroy intruders, so why had GrayCris hired someone else?

The obvious answer was that Wilken and Gerth weren't here to kill the team, but wanted to get into the terraforming facility because there was something, either data or a physical object, that they intended to retrieve. But they had made no move to retrieve anything. I was certain Wilken had been surprised by the combat bot attack, my analysis there was not faulty. Had Wilken and Gerth even been sent by GrayCris, or was there another corporate or political entity in play?

I needed help. I was rattled, I was still leaking a little, and I hadn't been able to watch any media in what felt like forever. In desperation, I copied all my possibilities into a potential strategy/decision tree diagram and threw it into the feed for Abene and Miki.

Abene winced, startled at the sudden large image in her feed. Then her face went still as she studied the diagram. Miki wiped wound sealant onto the last shrapnel laceration in my back and shifted into analysis mode. Hirune, still half conscious, watched us with a confused expression.

In the feed, Abene detached one of the assumption

squares and moved it away from the tree. She said, *If we assume Wilken and Gerth were sent by GrayCris, then they aren't here to retrieve anything. GrayCris had ample opportunity to remove anything they wanted when they abandoned the facility.* She hesitated, her attention moving from one assumption square to another. *I think we have to ask ourselves, what does GrayCris want?*

That was easy. I said, *To destroy the facility. If GoodNightLander Independent hadn't installed the tractor array, the facility would have collapsed into the planet by now.*

Abene's brow furrowed as she looked at the squares listing possible exit scenarios and the problems with each one. *So why weren't Wilken and Gerth sent to destroy the tractor array? Actually, perhaps they were.*

Miki said, aloud, "Wilken altered the flat display on her right forearm armor to show local facility time." It sent us an image in the feed: Wilken adjusting the display on her armor. The image had been captured when I asked Miki to look at the two security consultants as they stowed their equipment when the shuttle was getting ready to undock from the transit station. "She checked that display approximately fifty-seven times during our walk through the facility, until she attempted to hurt Don Abene."

I hadn't noticed that, but when I reran a portion of my video, there it was. Abene said slowly, "Wilken knew something would happen to the facility, and approximately when it would happen. She could only wait so long before she had to get back to the shuttle. When she had the opportunity, she sent you off to be killed by the combat bots, and intended to kill me and Miki. Then she would tell the others it was hopeless and force them to return to the transit station—"

The combat bots' behavior was starting to make sense. If they had been waiting for something, too, it explained why they had taken Hirune prisoner. They had assigned one bot to mess with us. To attack, grab a prisoner, retreat, attack again. I had destroyed it when it attacked Wilken, but the other three hadn't come rushing after us. Two had been in the engineering pod, and one was out of range, doing what?

Abene took a sharp breath. She said, "It has to be the tractor array. There's no other real benefit for GrayCris." In the feed, she flicked away the assumption squares for the actions of a theoretical station-bound GrayCris operative. "We know from the drone there is no controller for the combat bots, no one aboard the transit station sending orders to them. They are original equipment, meant to defend the facility until it collapsed naturally into the planet, leaving no evidence that it was an illegal mining operation. Wilken and Gerth didn't know about the bots and weren't sent to kill us, because killing us is not the goal. The goal is to let the facility be destroyed as planned. The thing that prevents the facility being destroyed is the tractor array. Therefore Wilken and Gerth were sent here to do something, and they thought the only consequence of that something was that the tractor array would fail, and we would be forced to leave the facility. We would all return to the transit station and they would leave aboard the next cargo ship, with no one the wiser." She slipped out of the feed and turned to me. "But what could they have done? They were with us the whole time."

I thought she was right, and there was only one thing they could have done without me or someone in the team noticing. "They sent an encrypted signal." A comm signal, not a feed signal. With all the storm interference, and more importantly the fact that I hadn't been looking for it, I had missed it.

"Yes, yes." Abene's brows lifted. "But to who? The combat bots? Is there a weapon, a way for the bots to destroy the array from here?" She turned to look at the other consoles.

I checked my connection to the shuttle's audio again. Kader was pushing Gerth about trying to go aboard the facility to search for the others, backed up by Brais and Vibol. No mention of any problem with the tractor array. They had to be monitoring it. Gerth was pushing back, saying they had to wait like they agreed. I ran the audio back. She wanted them to wait thirty minutes. The digger display sent a ping into the feed, indicating that the diggers had finished their full power-up. I sent the shuttle audio into the feed for Abene and Miki and sat down at the digger control station. Whatever was going to happen, it was going to be soon.

As I sent the first set of orders for three of the diggers, Abene said to Miki, "We need sensors. Check all the consoles. Anything in here will be pointed at the surface, but we can try to redirect—"

I backburnered everything but the diggers. Abene was obviously still interested in saving the facility, but my priority was in getting off the facility before it broke up in the atmosphere.

The three diggers uncoiled out of their housings and started to walk across the outside of the lower half of the geo pod. Their multiple arms gripped the surface securely as they moved, the cameras giving me a dizzying view of the storm. They didn't have the memory cores with their mining protocols, but then they wouldn't need them for what I wanted them to do.

Abene had booted another console and data popped up above the display surface as Miki leaned over it. Hirune shoved to her feet and limped over to them, leaning on the back of a chair.

I needed to copy over some specialized code from the console, but once I had it, I could control the three diggers through the feed. I assigned them yet another channel in my overworked brain, and stood up. Oh, okay, ouch. Without their protocols, controlling them was tricky. I basically had to drive all three of them at once. Keeping my voice level and patient, I said, "We need to go. You have six minutes."

Abene waved a hand. "We've almost got it."

I reminded myself I was still pretending to be a SecUnit under contract, and put the countdown in the feed with no additional commentary. Then I collected Wilken's weapon and harness and went to stand by the hatch.

Hirune looked around, picked up the emergency kit from where Miki had left it, and limped over to stand beside me. She was unsteady on her feet and still clearly a little out of it, but having been carried off by a combat bot once, she was obviously ready to call it a day.

Abene pushed to her feet. "Yes, there! Copy that trajectory, Miki." Miki acknowledged and followed Abene as she strode to the doorway. "Some sort of structure launched from the engineering pod and is heading toward the tractor array. The missing combat bot must be aboard it, and it means to destroy the array. Those orders must have been in the encrypted transmission Wilken and Gerth sent."

That's great! And I will care about the fucking tractor array once I get us on the fucking shuttle! Watching my own countdown, I pulled three inputs forward, my drone, Miki, and the diggers. No wait, I needed my own camera, too. Four inputs. Oh, and the suit audio from the shuttle. Five inputs. I had the drone do a quick check of the foyer and the access to the lift junction, making sure it was clear. I said, "We need to move fast. We don't know where the other combat bots are."

Abene nodded and gripped Hirune's arm. Hirune whispered, "Where are we going?"

Abene shushed her. "Back to the shuttle. It's all right." Miki patted Hirune's shoulder.

I hit the release for the hatch and stepped out. The fast walk to the lift junction made every nerve in my human skin itch. The drone scouted ahead of us, scanning, but I irrationally expected the bots to leap out from around the next corner.

We reached the junction and I sent the drone ahead in my invisible lift. Abene and Miki talked on the feed, occasionally making a reassuring comment to Hirune. They could be plotting to sell me for parts and I couldn't spare the attention to listen in. Outside the diggers neared the curve of the geo pod. They would need to follow the trough between it and the habitation pod to avoid being spotted by the shuttle.

The lift reached the junction nearest our docking area

and the drone zipped out. I sent it on a quick scouting pattern, up and down the access and through into the decontam room, then up to get a view of the shuttle's lock. The scan was clear, and I told the drone to return to the lift junction and hold position.

The lift returned and I got the humans inside. (And Miki, but at the moment I was classing it with the humans.) I directed the diggers to speed up a little. I wanted us to spend as little time in the access corridor to the shuttle as possible. If the combat bots decided we were putting their mission at risk, they'd come after us and they knew they could catch us there. As I started the lift, I sent Abene the diggers' video so she'd have some idea of what the shuttle was about to see, and told her, "When I unlock your feed, connect to Kader and tell him to make sure to get everyone off the shuttle."

"I will." She nodded sharply and squeezed Hirune's hand, and tapped Miki's feed.

The lift reached the junction and I was out as soon as the doors slid open. I moved toward the decontam room, the humans behind me, and I sent the diggers over the curve of the habitation pod and straight in toward the shuttle.

On board, through my connection to the evac suits on the flight deck, I heard Vibol say something in a language

I didn't have loaded, and Kader say, "We've got something approaching, unknowns are approaching—"

Distantly, from somewhere below the flight deck, Gerth shouted, "What? What direction?"

I opened Abene's feed connection, and told her, *Now*.

She made the private connection to Kader and said, *Kader, listen. No questions, don't tell anyone I'm here. You must get everyone off the shuttle into the facility now, at once. Do whatever you must, pretend to be in a panic, but get everyone off. Your lives depend on it.*

Through Abene's feed, I heard Kader trigger an emergency evacuate order that blared across the team's feed and the shuttle comms. Gerth had started up to the flight deck and snarled, "Stop, stop where—"

I thought she might trap Kader and Vibol in the cockpit, and we'd be back to a hostage situation. But Kader, who must have taken the "pretend to panic" advice to heart, sent the vid of the approaching diggers from the shuttle's sensors into the feed and screamed for the others to get out.

I reached the corridor and had a view of the docking chamber as the shuttle's hatch cycled open. Brais staggered out, a semi-conscious Ejiro leaning on her. Miki ran to help them, Abene hanging back with Hirune, and I followed.

I told one digger to let go of the facility's surface and

dive at the shuttle's nose, where the forward sensor would have the best view. Abene was in Kader's feed but with no cameras I got nothing but a confused jumble of impressions.

(I found out later from Gerth's armor cam that the sudden sensor view of something large coming at the shuttle had made Gerth jerk backward out of the flight deck access. Vibol, taking Kader's performance as evidence that the shuttle was about to be torn apart, grabbed Kader and dove past Gerth with him tucked under her arm, using the lighter gravity in the access to keep from slamming into the bulkhead. When they hit the corridor floor, they stumbled in the heavier gravity, staggered, and bolted for the hatch.)

Anyway, Kader and Vibol flung themselves out of the hatch, and Gerth, in her powered armor, strode out after them. I was standing to one side of the shuttle hatch by that point, so all Gerth saw was the others, confused and panicked, with Abene and Hirune, and a one-handed Miki holding up Ejiro.

I scanned her armor and found the right code. (It was a much quicker process now that I knew where to look.) Just as she brought her projectile weapon up, I sent the command.

Her armor froze in place, and I stepped around into view. Her expression as she realized what had happened was gratifying. If she had been using her scan, she would have detected me just outside the hatch, but even with the feed, even augmented, humans can only think about one thing at a time.

Abene said, "Now we must get back on the shuttle!"

The others demanded answers and she explained rapidly as she shooed them toward the hatch. I tuned it out to check on all my other inputs. Without my orders, the diggers had gone dormant and stopped where they were. Two were still on the surface of the habitation pod, and the one that had lifted off to dive at the shuttle had landed on the atmosphere pod. Then I checked the drone, which I had left in the lift junction to watch our backs.

It started to respond with a scan of the area, then the transmission cut off abruptly. I felt the connection drop, the drone going out like a light.

I said, "Abene, Miki, bots!" I crossed the room, pulling Wilken's projectile weapon off my back.

Abene yelled, "Aboard, now!"

I reached the doorway and started to pull explosive packs off Wilken's harness, arm them, and toss them down the corridor. I still had Miki's camera as an input and I backburnered it, but I was peripherally aware of the humans scrambling, getting the wounded Ejiro and Hirune through the lock, and Abene telling Miki to pick up Gerth and carry her in. It was about that time when the combat bot slammed around the corner and the first explosive charge went off.

I fired three projectiles, just to make it think I was going to stand here like an idiot and shoot at it, then sprinted back across the room. The charges in the corridor delayed the bot long enough for the humans and Miki to get Gerth in and clear the lock. I flung myself through and I hit the emergency close. Both hatches slammed down.

Finally, I had gotten these fucking people back on this fucking shuttle.

The combat bot hit the outer hatch with an impact like we had been rammed by another small shuttle. I sent to Abene, *We need to go.*

The clamps gave way and the shuttle fell away from the lock. I checked the camera view of the outer hatch and saw the combat bot standing in the open docking port, holding onto the sides as the chamber decompressed. There was a second one behind it. Miki stood beside me, and I shared the image with it on our feed connection. It said, "Those bots were mean, SecUnit."

I was losing the connection with distance but one of my diggers was close enough to the lock, crouched in sleep mode. I sent it a last order and it whipped its big hand down, snatched the first bot out of the port, and crushed it.

"Ouch," Miki commented. *SecUnit, why don't you talk to me on the feed anymore?*

Miki knew why, or it wouldn't have asked.

I stepped around it and went down the access corridor. Miki said in the feed, *I didn't tell on you until I had to.*

I went up the corridor toward the crew area. Miki picked up Gerth and followed. In the comm audio, I had been monitoring Abene while she gave the others the quick version of what had happened with Wilken, how I had saved Hirune, how Wilken had shot Miki's poor hand off, how I had saved her and Miki, and so on, whatever. I had my geo pod data for Dr. Mensah, I had saved Miki's stupid humans, I just wanted to get out of here. The shuttle was moving away from the facility and I could feel the transit station's feed just on the edge of my range.

I stepped into the crew area. Kader and Vibol were up in the cockpit, but the others were here, though Ejiro and Hirune were collapsed into seats. Ejiro looked woozy but more alert than Hirune, who probably needed to be stuffed into the MedSystem. Miki set Gerth on her feet, and everyone stared at her for a second, then at me.

Brais stood, facing the floating display. It showed a sensor view of the tractor array above the facility. "Yes, there it is. The object is heading toward the tractor array."

Abene looked grim. "We think it's a work zipper from the engineering pod. One of the combat bots is aboard."

I said, "Don Abene, we need to return to the transit station as soon as possible. When the tractor array fails, it could damage the shuttle." I guess it could. I don't know, it sounded good.

In my feed, Miki said, *I never talked to a bot like me before. I have human friends, but I never had a friend like me.*

I had to bite my cheek to keep my expression at SecUnit neutral. I wanted to block Miki's feed, but I needed to keep monitoring it in case the humans started plotting against me. (I know, it sounds paranoid. But Miki and Abene knew I'd made Consultant Rin up, and I needed to get away before they told that to a human who knew just how not normal that behavior was for a SecUnit.)

On the comm from the flight deck, Kader said, "We've got to commit in the next minute, are you sure about this?"

Wait, what? I ran back my recording and listened to Brais say, "We can use the shuttle to knock the zipper off course. Our shielding will protect our hull—"

Squinting at the display, Ejiro said, "But wouldn't the zipper be able to return and try again?"

Brais shook her head, still watching the flight projection. "I've pulled the specs on that model of zipper. It's meant for facility maintenance and needs a feed connection to the engineering pod to operate. We can push it out of range and it'll lose navigation control."

Oh, great. How long was that going to take?

By the time I caught up to realtime, they had already decided to do it, they were just arguing about specifics.

I stood there watching the glowing shapes on the display as Kader took the shuttle closer to the zipper. I admit, I did watch a little more of the episode I had paused while this was going on. (It was only six minutes, but it was a boring six minutes, okay? Also, Miki had walked over to stand sadly next to Abene and stare at me, and I was ignoring it. Abene thought Miki was sad about the missing hand, and kept patting it and telling it they would get it fixed as soon as they got back to the station.)

(It's a good thing I don't have a stomach and can't vomit.)

Finally the shuttle bumped the zipper off its course, dramatically saving the tractor array and GoodNightLander Independent's investment with forty-five seconds to spare, yay. The humans congratulated each other, and Abene and Brais helped Hirune stand so they could take her to the medical unit. There was still one combat bot left on the facility, but that sounded like somebody else's problem. The shuttle had altered course to head back to the station and we were close enough already for me to ping Ship through the feed. It pinged back, still waiting for me. That was a relief.

And I heard a clank from the hatch.

I'm not an expert on space, but I was pretty sure stuff wasn't supposed to knock on the hatch. It might have been debris from the zipper, but I knew. I just knew it wasn't. I checked the hatch camera, and got a wide-angle view of combat bot face.

The next connection overrode the station feed, temporarily blotting out all my channels: [*Objective: kill intruders.*]

Oh, shit.

I blocked the bot out of my feed and yelled, "Emergency! Lock breach imminent!" I sent the images from the hatch camera to Miki and through it into the rest of the team's feed. The humans froze and it felt like forever, it felt like they weren't going to believe me. But I had forgotten how slow humans seemed to move when I actually had all my attention on what I was doing. Kader hit the all-ship alarm and sealed the two interior hatches between the lock and the crew area. Great, that would buy me a minute, maybe two.

I told Abene, "Get everyone into the flight deck." There was another hatch there and it might buy another minute. I turned for the access to the compartment just below us where Gerth and Wilken had stored their gear.

As I climbed out of the access I heard Abene yelling, "Go, go," and I knew from the team feed that the shuttle was heading toward the station and Vibol was tersely explaining to the Port Authority that we were about to be torn apart by a combat bot.

(Frankly, I didn't know what station security was going to do about it, either. In fact, I'm sure station security was now shitting itself almost as hard as I metaphorically was.)

The hatch camera helpfully showed me the outer hatch being punched apart, then the feed fizzled and died. The bot would be working on the first inner hatch now. I reached the compartment and saw that Wilken and Gerth had left one case beside the empty ones that had held their armor, the large projectile weapons, explosive packs, and ammo. I tore the remaining case open and found another set of small charges, the kind used more for getting through security doors and hatches. There was a bag that felt empty when I grabbed it and I used it to scoop up the charges and some extra ammo for the projectile weapon I had across my back. It wasn't going to be that helpful since I doubted I'd have time to use it. Maybe I should have spent the time trying to set up a position instead of coming down here hoping for a decent bot-busting weapon. In the bot-fighting business, small mistakes like that get you torn apart.

In the feed, I heard Abene and Brais handing Hirune up the access to the cockpit. They had already got Ejiro up there. In my feed, Miki said, *Hurry, hurry.* Abene had told it to bring Gerth and it was holding her. The combat bot pounded on the hatch to the crew area. I shoved upright, turned, and that's when I saw the assessment team's equipment storage.

There were cases and racks of environmental testing and sampling tools. One was a core cutter, made to take nice round cylinders out of walls of rock for whatever reason humans need to do that. It was an extension meant to attach to a sampler unit, but they probably had it because Miki was strong enough to lift it and use it; it's a long tube that uses directed explosive cutters to extract meter-length sections.

I slung the ammo bag over my back, grabbed the cutter off the rack, switched on its power pack, and climbed up the access.

I stepped back into the crew area just as Miki flung Gerth after Abene and hit the manual seal for the hatch. It dropped and Miki turned. I told it, *Miki, get out of here! Go hide in the cargo!*

No, Rin, it said, *I'm going to help you!*

In the feed, Abene yelled at Miki to come in with them, she would tell Kader to open the hatch if it would just come in—and Miki told her, *Priority is to protect my friends.*

Priority change, Abene sent. *Priority is to protect yourself.*

That priority change is rejected, Miki told her.

The core cutter had powered up and accessed my feed

to deliver a canned warning and a handy set of directions. Why yes, I did want to disengage the safety protocols, thanks for asking.

I'd meant to give the core cutter to Miki so it could get the combat bot while I distracted it. But the combat bot blew the hatch and was suddenly in the crew area with us, and there was no time for a plan, no time for strategy.

The bot knew I was there and it turned, reaching for me as I lifted the cutter. Miki braced its feet against the hatch protecting the flight deck access and pushed off. It launched across the cabin, its body cutting through the floating display, straight at the combat bot's head. I don't know if Miki was trying to distract the combat bot, or if it had seen me make a similar attack on the bot that came after Wilken, and was trying to duplicate the technique. Air rushed out of the pressurized cabin, down the access corridor and out the ruined airlock, and as Miki jumped the flow gave it an extra boost of speed.

The bot caught the motion and turned away from me, lifted up and extended an arm to catch Miki by the torso. I took the opening and lunged in to slam the core cutter right against the bot's side, where its brain was. I triggered the cutter. I didn't have time to brace myself, and the recoil knocked me backward and for three seconds my vision went black.

I was flat on the deck, and all I could hear in the feed

was humans yelling from the cockpit, humans yelling over the comm from the Port Authority, and the shuttle's emergency siren making sure everyone knew the air had just explosively vacated due to lock breaches. The core cutter was on top of me and I pushed it off and sat up. I knew at some point I had heard Abene scream in anguish, but I wasn't sure when it had happened.

The combat bot still stood, but it was unmoving, joints frozen. The core cutter had gone through its torso from one side to the other and extracted a neat cross-section of the protective shielding and the bot's processors. The core had been ejected from the back of the cutter and had fallen to the deck. I realized that was what had hit me in the head. I guess despite the instructions I had been holding it wrong.

Miki was crumpled in front of the bot, and something looked wrong. I was climbing to my feet, trying to see how Miki was damaged, when I froze. Something looked wrong because Miki's chest was crushed, its processor, memory, everything that made it Miki squeezed to nothing in one flex of the combat bot's hand.

I just sat on the deck. The shuttle neared the station, and the humans were on the comm, talking to the PA from the cockpit. They couldn't lower the flight deck hatch because of the lock breaches, and I hadn't answered their attempts to call me on feed or comm. I had still been sending visuals from my camera to the team feed, and they had seen the fight and Miki's last moment from my point of view. Before I cut my feed connection to them, I'd heard Abene sobbing, Hirune trying to comfort her, the others murmuring in shock.

I need air, too, though not nearly as much as humans, and maybe the lack of it was what made me feel so slow and disconnected. I used the station feed to ping Ship again and told it to unlock from the station, and I gave it a rendezvous position. Its calm acknowledgement felt strange, like everything was normal and nothing disastrous had happened.

Vibol knocked on the other side of the flight deck hatch, calling, "SecUnit, are you there? Please answer!"

I needed to get out of here. I shoved to my feet and went down the corridor to the emergency suit locker. I put on a full evac suit with maneuvering jets and the burst of air once I got the helmet sealed made me feel more alert. I made sure to leave the locker open and unclamp the other suits, so when anyone noticed one was missing, they would assume it had happened during the attack and the suit had been drawn out with the other debris. I wanted them to think that that was what had happened to me, that I had been sucked out of the lock in pieces. Then I went down the corridor to the ruined lock, pulled myself out and away.

I hadn't used a suit like this before (they don't generally let murderbots float around in space unsupervised) but the internal instruction feed was very helpful. By the time Ship arrived, I was able to jet into its airlock like a pro.

To the station, it would have looked like Ship had paused to let the shuttle get past so it could safely dock at the PA's slot. I didn't think anybody would be looking at the sensors for escaping SecUnits in evac suits.

Once I'd cycled through the lock and had Ship crank up its air system a little, I told it to proceed on its usual course for the wormhole and HaveRatton Station. I got the suit off, dumped it aside with Wilken's weapon and the ammo bag I had grabbed out of the case. I sat down on the deck and started methodically checking all the equipment to make sure there were no tracers.

Abene had tried to change Miki's priority to saving its own life, and it had refused her. Which meant she had allowed its programming that option, that ability to use its own judgment in a crisis situation. It had decided its priority was to save its humans, and maybe to save me, too. Or maybe it had known it couldn't save any of us, but it had wanted to give me the chance to try. Or it hadn't wanted me to face the bot alone. Whatever it was, I'd never know.

What I did know was that Abene really had loved Miki. That hurt in all kinds of ways. Miki could never be my friend, but it had been her friend, and more importantly, she had been its friend. Her gut reaction in a moment of crisis was to tell Miki to save itself.

After I checked the charges and ammo in the bag, I found a fake pocket in the bottom. Inside it were several sets of identity markers and a larger, different brand of memory clip from the ones I had stored in my arm. I heaved myself upright, and found a reader in the cargo console.

Well, that was interesting.

I hate caring about stuff. But apparently once you start, you can't just stop.

I wasn't going to just send the geo pod data to Dr. Mensah. I was taking it to her personally. I was going back.

Then I laid down on the floor and started *Rise and Fall of Sanctuary Moon* from episode one.

About the Author

MARTHA WELLS has written many fantasy novels, including *The Wizard Hunters, Wheel of the Infinite*, the Books of the Raksura series (beginning with *The Cloud Roads*), and the Nebula-nominated *The Death of the Necromancer*, as well as YA fantasy novels, short stories, and nonfiction. She has had stories in *Black Gate, Realms of Fantasy, Stargate* magazine, *Lightspeed* magazine, and in the anthologies *Elemental, Tales of the Emerald Serpent, The Other Half of the Sky, The Gods of H. P. Lovecraft*, and *MECH: Age of Steel*. She has also written media tie-ins for *Stargate: Atlantis* and most recently *Star Wars: Razor's Edge*. The last book in the Books of the Raksura series, *The Harbors of the Sun*, was released in July 2017.